Who was he...and what did he want with her?

Sheera had always liked the Ambassador Hotel—but never in her wildest dreams had she thought she'd be held prisoner there.

Yet now she was being ushered into the lobby by someone who had suddenly become either her jailer or her protector. Common sense sparred with growing panic. She didn't know what to believe.

"Where are you taking me?" she demanded.

"To my room," the man called Damien answered easily. His expression was purposely blank. "You're not in any danger from me, so don't worry."

But Sheera had just been chased through the park by two men—and only because of her encounter with Damien—so how could she *not* worry...?

ABOUT THE AUTHOR

Marie Nicole began her writing career at the age of eleven. She is the author of many romance novels. Married to a man she has known since the tenth grade, Marie lives with him and their two children in California.

Books by Marie Nicole
HARLEQUIN INTRIGUE
21–THICK AS THIEVES
30–CODE NAME: LOVE

These books may be available at your local bookseller.

Don't miss any of our special offers. Write to us at the following address for information on our newest releases.

Harlequin Reader Service
P.O. Box 52040, Phoenix, AZ 85072-2040
Canadian address: P.O. Box 2800, Postal Station A,
5170 Yonge St., Willowdale, Ont. M2N 6J3

CODE NAME: LOVE
MARIE NICOLE

Harlequin Books

TORONTO • NEW YORK • LONDON
AMSTERDAM • PARIS • SYDNEY • HAMBURG
STOCKHOLM • ATHENS • TOKYO • MILAN

To my mom,
who always loved a good adventure story
And to my dad,
who filled in the gaps for me
*Dla Mamy i Taty,
od Marysi*

Harlequin Intrigue edition published November 1985

ISBN 0-373-22030-8

Copyright © 1985 Marie Rydzynski-Ferrarella. All rights reserved.
Philippine copyright 1985. Australian copyright 1985.
Except for use in any review, the reproduction or utilization of
this work in whole or in part in any form by any electronic,
mechanical or other means, now known or hereafter invented,
including xerography, photocopying and recording, or in any
information storage or retrieval system, is forbidden without
the permission of the publisher, Harlequin Enterprises Limited,
225 Duncan Mill Road, Don Mills, Ontario Canada M3B 3K9, or
Harlequin Books, P.O. Box 958, North Sydney, Australia 2060.

All the characters in this book have no existence outside the
imagination of the author and have no relation whatsoever to
anyone bearing the same name or names. They are not even
distantly inspired by any individual known or unknown to the
author, and all incidents are pure invention.

The Harlequin trademark, consisting of the words
HARLEQUIN INTRIGUE, with or without the portrayal of a
Harlequin, are trademarks of Harlequin Enterprises Limited;
the portrayal of a Harlequin is registered in the
United States Patent and Trademark Office and in the
Canada Trade Marks Office.

Printed in Canada

Chapter One

Boredom, Sheera O'Malley thought as she held on to an overhead strap in an elevated train, was a terrible thing. It seeped into your veins slowly, like molasses; it colored your entire life and took the joy out of everything.

The heavy rumbling gave way to a high-pitched screech as the train jolted to a stop at the Roosevelt Avenue station. But the doors stood still, like a stubborn child refusing to do what was asked of him. A crescendo of annoyed grumbling arose in the train as the Monday morning travelers, already weary with the thought of the week that lay before them, began to lose their patience.

"C'mon already, quit stallin'. Open the damn doors," a burly man who was standing in front of one of the sets of double doors growled. Pounding accompanied the demand.

Sheera shook her head. Eight o'clock in the morning was awfully early for frustration to set in. But she felt it herself.

Finally, the graffiti-splattered doors yawned open—except for the ones nearest her, which remained obstinately shut. Obscenities littered the air as people intent on changing trains at the Roosevelt Avenue station burrowed their way to the nearest open doors, pushing their bulk against passengers who refused to move. Another gladiatorial contest was under way, one of many that took place within the New York City subways every day.

It was Sheera's stop as well, but even if it hadn't been, she doubted she could have stayed on. The tide of people around her literally swept her up and took her with them. She made it through the door just as it began to close. She felt the black rubber on the door hungrily clamp down, as it shut, against the heel of her shoe. It also snared the edge of her new beige spring suit. Sheera gave a mighty yank, separating herself from the mechanical monster before it lumbered on its way to the next stop.

Sheera pulled the hem of her skirt around and looked down. A black mark ran along the length of it, a souvenir of combat. "Terrific," she muttered. "And so starts another wonderful week."

She joined the flow of bodies hurrying down the long, narrow stairs that led from the brisk outer, elevated world, where one could see the sky and treetops, down into the dirty, dark bowels of the multilevel station. All levels were teeming with people.

Mondays were always the hardest to bear. There were always more people out on Monday. Absently, Sheera wondered why. Maybe they couldn't take it for more than one day.

There were people everywhere—students clutching books, on their way to college; people off to work—all like dutiful ants. And she was one of them.

The escalator to the street level lay like an immobile giant, its iron stairs frozen. People clattered down uneasily, as if expecting it to rise up and move at any moment. Sheera held on to the handrail and made her way down as quickly as possible. The sound of a train arriving at the station below drowned out any scraps of the disgruntled conversation that was buzzing around her. She hurried down the last flight of stairs. But the train that was undergoing an exchange of passengers was going in the opposite direction of her destination.

Sheera sighed. Why was she hurrying? She was an hour early as it was. She didn't have to be at her job until after nine. Restless, she ran her hand through her shoulder-length copper-colored hair. That restlessness had prompted her to go to the hairdresser last Saturday and ask for a make-over, then had made her agree to spend that weekend with her younger sister and her family in Jackson Heights. She knew she was searching for something, but she didn't know what it was.

Sheera wandered over to a small, cluttered newsstand. The unkempt man who sat in the eight-by-four box seemed content enough, she thought, struck by the irony of it. He sat, apparently satisfied, in a claustrophobic box on a subway platform all day long, while she was unhappy with a high-profile, well-paid career. The thought didn't help her any. She shook her head.

An array of current magazines, held in place by tiny clamps, bordered the top of the newsstand, their neatness in stark contrast to the slovenliness of the proprietor. The headline on a bright yellow cover caught her eye momentarily: "What to Do about Mid-life Crisis When It Strikes."

Sheera smiled despite herself. It was too soon for her mid-life crisis. She was only thirty. And vice-president of Starlight Cosmetics, Inc.

And bored.

Without thinking, she took down the magazine with the bright yellow cover and stared at it. Who would have ever thought that success could be boring? Certainly not she. Not when she had started out, anyway. She had always been the ambitious one in her family. She had graduated with an M.B.A. from Cornell University, complete with honors. Her father had always referred to her as the go-getter. Well, the go-getter had gone and gotten all the things she had been after and was now experiencing a gnawing, vague dissatisfaction. But dissatisfaction with what? She wasn't even sure—perhaps with life in general.

Was this all there was to life?

She had never before indulged in self-pity, and now she was suddenly wallowing in it. What was wrong with her?

She should be ashamed of herself, Sheera thought as she watched a bag lady shuffle along. All the woman's tattered belongings had been shoved into two overflowing shopping bags that threatened to break apart at any minute. Her body was covered with layers of clothing as if to ward off the cold permanently, in any season.

What if life had dealt her a hand like that, Sheera upbraided herself, her fingers curling around the magazine she had absently picked up from the newsstand. She was lucky to be where she was, to have been born who she was, with opportunities open to her and with a warm, loving, indulgent family who had never held her back. "So why don't I feel lucky?" she muttered, annoyed.

She watched the bag lady shuffle along, asking for money. People pretended not to notice her, turning their backs before she reached them, or shifting their attention to that morning's news neatly laid out within the pages of *The New York Times* and the *Daily News*.

Except for one man, a tall, bearded man in a well-tailored blue-gray suit. He wasn't more than ten feet away, and Sheera was able to look on, hidden by the crowd, while the bag lady pathetically tugged at the sleeve of his expensive suit. Instead of curtly sending the woman on her way, however, the man smiled, a genial, compassionate smile. The smile of a man with a heart, Sheera mused. He put his hand into his pocket and gave the disheveled woman whatever he drew out. He didn't even look to see if it was a dollar or a bill of some higher denomination, Sheera observed, surprised.

The bag lady walked past her. One grimy hand pushed aside the plastered, dirty hair, momentarily raising it from her eyes. Sheera was taken aback to see that the face peering at her was young. How long could she have been a bag lady, Sheera wondered. It couldn't have been all that long. The woman's eyebrows were carefully shaped and plucked. Sheera had spent too much time under the strict dictates of perfect grooming not to have noticed that about the woman immediately.

Her curiosity aroused, Sheera unconsciously took a step to follow the bag woman.

"Hey, lady, you buyin' or rentin'?" The gravelly voice snapped at her, bringing her attention back to the newsstand. Sheera looked at the stoop-shouldered man standing within the magazine-cluttered enclosure. His small eyes were glaring accusingly at the magazine in her hand.

She couldn't really blame him. He probably lost several pieces of merchandise every day to nimble-fingered passersby. But she didn't like his tone of voice, and her annoyed look told him so. "I'm buying," she said tartly.

The bearded stranger was watching her, she realized. There was a twinkle in his eyes, which she could see even at that distance. As she took out her change purse from her shoulder bag, she left the bag open for a moment. Just as she reached out to pay for the magazine, she was jostled from behind by a burly teenager in a dirty pea-green Windbreaker.

"Excuse *me*!" she said curtly as the teenager kept loping on his way.

She saw the stranger with the beard turn and match the teenager's gait, heading in the same direction. She thought it odd that he seemed to be in such a hurry when, a moment ago, he had looked content to stand by the iron pillar idly waiting for a train. Well, that was no concern of hers. A lot of strange things went on underground every day.

"Here," Sheera said to the newsstand operator, counting out a dollar and fifty cents in change and laying the coins flat on a towering pile of newspapers. She didn't really want the magazine, but she wanted a hassle even less.

She heard the sound of raised voices not far from where she was standing, but because of the noise level in the train station, she couldn't make out what was being said. *Tempers get raw when you have to travel in sardine cans,* she thought, shoving the magazine under her arm.

She realized that her bag was still hanging open and was about to put her change purse back in when she noticed that her shoulder bag wasn't as full as it had been a second ago. Her heart thumped hard as she realized what was missing.

Her wallet!

Immediately she looked in the direction in which the teenager had gone. He had taken it! "Damn!" she swore loudly.

The remark went unnoticed by the people around her. Even the newsstand operator ignored her.

What a horrid way to start Monday morning, she thought. There was no way she would ever find that kid, not in this crowd.

Sheera pressed her lips together. Nothing to do except to go on to work and call the police when she got there. Fat lot of good that would do, she fumed. How many wallets were stolen every day?

She felt her ire rising. Well, now she wasn't bored anymore, she told herself wryly. Now she was mad.

"You really should be more careful, you know."

Her temper raw, Sheera swung around to tell the busybody to mind his own business, even though she had no idea what had prompted that remark. But the words died in her throat when she recognized the man with the beard. He was holding her wallet up like a bagged trophy.

Sheera took it from him, surprised beyond words. "How did you...?"

"I saw him bump you. Old trick. New around here?" he asked.

She liked his voice. Deep, resonant, cultured. It suited him. "No, I—"

"Then you should know better," he told her with a smile. Then, with a nod of his head, he simply walked away.

Sheera was left standing with her mouth hanging open—at least, figuratively. He hadn't even waited for her to say thank-you. She saw him take more or less the same position he'd had before he'd gone off in pursuit of the teenager.

What a strange man, she thought.

Strange, but handsome. As a rule, she didn't care for beards, even small ones. Beards were meant to hide imperfections. They hid a man's face from her, and she liked to see a person's features. She was in charge of the advertising campaigns at Starlight, so she had developed a keen eye for detail. She decided that the stranger's Van Dyke displayed more than it hid. It gave him a rather roguish appeal. That same mischievous look could be seen in the set of his mouth and in the twinkle of his sky-blue eyes. Even in the dim underground lighting, Sheera could see that there was more than a hint of amusement in them—amusement not at her folly for standing with a purse dangling open in the middle of a busy subway station, but at life in general. He looked like a man who enjoyed life. Watching him, she wondered what he did for a living.

The F train rumbled into the station, preceded by a burst of wind produced by the approach of the monstrous form. The train was one of the new ones the city had recently purchased. The doors opened and a sea of people flooded the cars. Some standees scrambled for the few seats that had been vacated by disembarking passengers. Sheera didn't even try to find a seat. She went directly to one of the central poles, claiming a small space for herself. Within moments, the pole was totally ringed by a motley collection of men and women. The man next to her insisted on reading his *Times*, shoving the huge paper almost under her nose.

Restlessness and dissatisfaction again took hold of her. Maybe it *did* have something to do with turning thirty, she thought. She had reached a pinnacle, a plateau, and she felt empty. There was no one special with whom to share things. She had never particularly wanted a home and family as her younger sister, Judy, had.

Sheera remembered her parents' marriage. Though they were both gone now, they had made an indelible impression on her because of their life together, an example of perfect domestic bliss. Never was a raised voice or a harsh, cutting word heard throughout her childhood; she had lived in an utterly orderly, serene atmosphere.

But that very perfection, the sheer monotonousness of such a life had signaled, at least to Sheera, that something was lacking. So she had gone off in the opposite direction. Her mother had been a professional wife and mother; Sheera wanted to be a professional career woman. She wanted to do something challenging, to find fulfillment in overcoming obstacles.

And at first, putting her M.B.A. degree to use at Starlight Cosmetics *had* been a challenge. But soon her achievements came too easily, and all the fun, Sheera realized, was gone.

The week before, she had just finished a particularly grueling campaign at work, and that Friday, instead of feeling victorious, she was left feeling utterly hollow. Rethinking her earlier goals, she faced the possibility that she may have wanted the wrong things. Maybe, in devoting herself exclusively to a career, she had fought against her true calling. So she had taken Judy up on her invitation to spend the weekend at her house, to evaluate what she was missing. It was a hellish weekend.

The experience was still fresh in her mind, like a newly painted room, full of dampness and smells. Little Kirby had provided the dampness and her brother-in-law, Steven, had provided the overwhelming smells with his ever-present pipe.

After two days with them, Sheera still did not know what it was she wanted, but she did know what she *didn't* want. She didn't want a marriage like Judy's. Or like her parents', either. Judy's family life was too hectic, too disorganized; her parents' lives had been too pat, too predictable. Both made her feel trapped.

She had made her escape very early this morning, leaving a hasty note to Judy about having to attend an early meeting. There was no early meeting—but Sheera had had to get out of there. The atmosphere was stifling.

So, she thought, *is this train ride.* She ducked her head away from the man with the newspaper and felt as if she had just been stabbed. "Ouch!"

The woman next to her was knitting. How she managed to keep her balance on the swaying train amazed Sheera. But the woman kept right on adding row upon row of wool to the garment growing beneath her fingers, yanking on the white yarn that was tucked into a large plastic purse slung over her arm. "Sorry," the woman finally muttered.

Sheera nodded in reply.

So, what do *you want,* she asked herself, for the umpteenth time, turning away from the woman and her lightning-fast knitting needles. A change. A change was in order. But what kind of a change? Did she want to give up her job after all? No, not really, she decided. Maybe all she needed was to get away, to go on a vacation. She hadn't taken one in years, always putting it off because of some large campaign or other that was being launched.

Well, it was high time *she* was launched, she thought. Maybe she should go on a long, lazy cruise. Who knew? Maybe she'd find out what was causing her dissatisfaction. Or at the very least, maybe she'd miss her job and learn to appreciate what she had.

Maybe...

Sheera's thoughts stopped short. He was in the same car—the stranger with the beard. She felt her interest stirring again, felt herself perking up slightly. He was watching her. Sheera caught herself smiling. And he smiled in return. He had a beautiful smile, beard or no beard. It made her feel warm, bright, inexplicably happy, like a cat out in the noonday sun.

Flirting, that's what she was doing. Flirting on the F train bound for Sixth Avenue. She hadn't flirted in years. Maybe *that* was what was wrong with her. She didn't necessarily need a husband, but she did need male attention. Exciting male attention. Something told her that this man was very exciting.

She was probably just attracted by the lure of the unknown, she told herself. All the men in her life had been as predictable, as staunchly stable, as her father. Three-piece, button-down predictable.

He was wearing a three-piece suit. He was facing her and she had a clear view of him. He was probably as predictable as the rest.

But somehow, Sheera doubted it.

These thoughts occupied her during the long ride through the tunnel and for the next two stops on the line. The train came to a halt at Rockefeller Center.

To her surprise, the stranger with the beard nodded a good-bye in her direction as he got off.

To her greater surprise, Sheera got off after him, two stops ahead of her own, ducking through the doors just as the closing bell sounded.

Chapter Two

Sheera was amazed—utterly and totally amazed. Sheera Teresa O'Malley, vice-president of Starlight Cosmetics, stalking a man? Yet here she was, briskly pushing her way through the crowd, trying to keep a bearded stranger in a designer suit in sight.

She continued to fight against the endless tide of people who were as equally determined to go down the subway stairs as she was to go up. It was difficult to be different from the masses in this city.

There should be some system to all this, she thought in annoyance, pressing herself against the banister as she inched along, step by step. Orderliness and precision had become quite important to her in the past few years. Of late, she had grown totally predictable. Well, she was certainly acting out of character for a change. This unexpected adventure suddenly made her feel like the vibrant young girl with dreams she had once been, a person she had missed being, she realized.

I just want to see where a man like that works, she told herself. But somehow she felt that something more would happen. She felt it in her bones.

You really do need a vacation.

But she kept on, driven by whimsy, desperation, instinct or a combination of all three. She wasn't sure anymore what was motivating her; she just knew that she needed a break in her routine. A new hairdo and a weekend with Judy and her family hadn't helped. Maybe satisfying her curiosity about the Good Samaritan with the beard would give her the boost she needed. In any event, that morning she had noticed that it was one of those rare, lovely spring days that should be savored, with a light blue sky punctuated by puffs of almost translucent white clouds. *A good day for a walk*, she told herself as she arrived at the top of the stairs leading to the long exit tunnel. It would seem a shame to waste such a glorious day, only seeing it filtered through the twenty-first-story window of her office.

Nevertheless, conscience urged her to forget about her walk and get back on the train to go to work. But instead of listening to her common sense, she rebelled. She was tired of being sensible, of being dependable.

Bodies jostled one another as they hurried along. Where was he? She stayed fixed, scanning the area.

"Damn tourists," a woman grumbled, shoving Sheera aside. "Pick some other place to do your gawking."

Holding back a retort, Sheera stepped aside and was bumped by several people as they hurried toward the Forty-seventh Street exit. Sheera's hand mechanically tightened around her shoulder bag. She thought of the stranger's bright blue eyes as he smiled at her when he handed back her wallet. Well, wherever he was now, he— She stopped. There he was, walking toward the Fifty-second Street exit!

Without thinking, Sheera began to hurry through the long, gray corridor. At both ends of the vast area, brightly lit stores displayed a variety of wares, from flowers and greeting cards to newspapers, posters and the like. Between the two extreme ends, however, the tunnel was essentially barren, marked only by equidistant stairwells that led to the trains below.

Sheera felt the rumble of a train beneath her feet. She kept her eyes on the stranger.

This is crazy, absolutely crazy, she thought. *What's the matter with you?* But she couldn't stop now. It was a game, something to dispel momentarily the overwhelming boredom she was drowning in.

DAMIEN CONRAD WAS AWARE of the woman behind him. He was too good an agent not to be. Eyes in the back of your head, that was the first requirement for his kind of work, wasn't it? He grinned.

He would have noticed her even if she hadn't been behaving peculiarly. He had noticed her as soon as she had descended the stairs at the Roosevelt Avenue station. There had been a momentary break in bodies and, as he had casually looked up the stairs, he was entranced by the sight of long, luscious legs, legs that could have modeled silk stockings back in the days when stockings had been made of silk. He was instantly fascinated and had waited to see if the rest of her matched her legs.

It did. She stood out in a crowd. The other people at the station blended into the endless sea of humanity that ebbed and flowed at each stop during the churning turmoil that was rush hour. She definitely stood out.

It wasn't her expensive-looking suit, or even that fiery-colored hair that swirled about her shoulders like a copper cloud, that impressed him. It was her face. It was a face he would have wanted to get to know better, if time had permitted. There was class there in those finely sculptured planes. Breeding—that was it. For a moment, just for a moment, she had taken his breath away.

Just the kind of woman *they* might use. Just the kind of woman to be leery of.

He had told himself that he had been at his job too long. After all, most people weren't part of "them" or "us"; they were just part of the humdrum world they lived in, going along, ignorant of the high drama that went on, unobserved, under their very noses.

Her place in the order of things had been established for him when that pickpocket had stolen her wallet. But then, maybe it had been too easy. Maybe it *had* been a setup, to distract him. The youth had been rather clumsy about it. And she had been unbelievably naive.

Still, she hadn't tried to engage him in any sort of conversation, and that spoke well for her, even though it had piqued his masculinity a little.

But there was the way she had scrutinized Cari. Had the titian-haired woman seen beyond Cari's tattered disguise? Had she realized that he had passed Cari a note telling Murphy to go ahead with the plan?

He was growing paranoid in his old age. The woman with the copper hair hadn't tried to pursue Cari in any fashion. And as far as he could tell, she hadn't signaled anyone, either.

Okay, if she was so innocent, what was she doing following him now?

Maybe she works around here, he thought irritably. Thousands of people filled this area every day. She was probably just a harmless woman who worked in one of the towering steel giants that proliferated in the area.

Maybe.

But somehow he wasn't all that certain. His instincts had managed to pull him through several tight spots in the past six years. He didn't like going against them. And his instincts told him she was following him.

He rubbed his beard. His chin itched. He wasn't used to facial hair, but it was necessary in this case. He couldn't wait to shave it off.

First, find Wawelski; then think about your pretty face, he admonished himself.

What if the woman was with the KGB? What if...? He stopped himself. It was too late now. He'd have to play it by ear, just as he had done so many other times. Plans, he had come to realize, had a way of falling apart in his line of work. Actually, that suited him fine; he liked to improvise. It made his job all the more exciting. It wasn't so much his sense of patriotism that kept him doing this kind of work as his sense of adventure. The challenge and the danger exhilarated him; it was a stimulant, a natural high.

He neared the Fifty-second Street exit, passing by the empty window of an abandoned store. He glanced at the window, pretending to smooth down his hair.

There she was.

Damien could see her walking briskly. She was definitely looking in his direction. Another man might have thought she was merely interested in a casual flirtation. She had caught his eye in the train and had given him a very warm smile. Damien was well aware of his good looks, but he had never let his self-confidence cloud his perception of the facts.

Was she an agent, he wondered again. He was beginning to think so. Was she one of theirs, or sent by some adjunct department within his own agency? That he couldn't be certain of—not yet, at any rate. All he knew was that she was being pretty obvious about it. If she *was* an agent, she definitely needed to be retrained or she would get herself killed. It would be a shame to lose someone as stunning as she was, no matter whose side she was on. Women like that certainly didn't come along every day.

HE WAS MOVING awfully slowly, Sheera thought as she watched him approach a shoeshine stand. It was getting hard not to look obvious, even among that crowd of people.

Now he had come to a total halt, she noticed in exasperation. She stopped, too, feeling a little foolish. *Forget this whole thing! Go back before he turns around and sees you acting like Nancy Drew and makes you feel like a total idiot.*

But she stood where she was.

The shoeshine stand was deserted. Why was he stopping there? There was no attendant to shine his shoes. She waited as Damien placed the attaché case he was carrying on the ground in order to tie his shoe. He was wearing old-fashioned shoes with laces.

He's probably just another stodgy three-piece suit, worried about stock options and retirement benefits. Get back on the damn F train and act sensibly before the men in the white coats come after you.

Sheera was about to turn and follow her own good advice when she saw another man approach the shoeshine stand, a man who looked exactly like her Good Samaritan. He had on the same type of suit and was wearing the same kind of beard. What a weird coincidence. Standing next to each other like that they might have been taken for twins from a distance. They probably didn't even realize it, she thought. Neither man looked in the other's direction.

See, there are plenty of men like that in New York, plenty of three-piece suits with shoes that lace up and lives that are buttoned down. A cruise is your only hope.

Deflated, she turned, heading for the stairs leading to the trains.

She turned back to take one last look at the man who might have become an adventure for her and saw the second man put his own attaché case next to the other. *Lemming,* she thought disparagingly.

The second man put a coin into the gum machine while her Good Samaritan, having finished tying his shoe, picked up his attaché case and continued on his way. As did the second man. Except that they had confused their attaché cases.

None of your business, Sheera. Go to work.

She took two steps toward the stairs. But he *had* rescued her wallet, she reminded herself. She was always ranting about how egocentric New Yorkers were, how they didn't want to get involved. She owed him something, didn't she?

"Excuse me!" Sheera called after the man.

He didn't hear her. Or if he did, he paid no attention. Her voice was swallowed up in the guttural rumblings of still another approaching train below.

Sheera quickened her pace. Didn't the idiot know that he had the wrong case? Of course not; the second man had placed his own case right next to her Good Samaritan's.

She had enough vacation time stored up to spend a month away from her job. A month on a cruise, or on some Pacific Island. It would do her good, she argued with herself.

Still, something compelled her to go on. The first man with the beard picked up his pace. She increased hers. Why was he moving so fast? Maybe she should just give up.

But her conscience pricked her. He had gone out of his way to retrieve her wallet; the least she could do was to tell him that he had picked up the wrong case. Maybe he had an important report in it, or documents that he needed. He'd be awfully upset to discover that they were gone.

"Excuse me!" Sheera called again. Damn it, why didn't he slow down?

Two men materialized from the shadows—or, more accurately, from among the milling crowds of commuters. Sheera saw them attach themselves to either side of her helpful stranger. Their pace never broke.

Now you can make a fool of yourself in front of three people instead of one, Sheera thought.

She stopped. This was ridiculous. She had her job to think of. It wasn't as if she hadn't tried to help him. And even if she caught up to him now, the other man was long gone. This whole thing was really rather silly, on her part anyway....

Why were they walking to that empty store at the side, she wondered. Tucked away from the main flow of foot traffic, the store had once been a seedy, little-used hot-dog stand, as she recalled. Why would he want to go there?

But as she moved closer, she realized that her Good Samaritan seemed to be hustled along by the two men against his will and that they were forcing him into the store's entrance. She was surprised that the door opened. Didn't someone usually lock up vacant stores to keep out vandals?

Her curiosity fully aroused, Sheera approached the store. Maybe he was a businessman scouting out locations for franchises. If that were the case, he certainly had poor judgment. Or maybe he really didn't want the store and the two men were pressuring him to consider it. They were probably the actual owners of the property.

Once again, she tried to tell herself that none of this was her business and that she should just go on to work. Oh, well, she had come this far. She might as well just pop in, tell the man with the beard that he had the wrong case and be on her way. Then, at least, her conscience would be clear. And, just maybe, an introduction would be in the offing.

Sheera hesitantly put her hand on the door, then swung it open. She bumped into something heavy.

"Psiakrew!"

She heard the curse just as she realized that she had bumped into someone. The apology on her lips vanished as she saw a gun fly by, landing on the floor inside the store. The next thing she knew, her Good Samaritan, looking rather stunned, came bolting out, grabbing her hand as he passed her.

"Who the hell *are* you?" he demanded, pulling her after him.

"Sheera O'Malley," she cried, confused. Why was he dragging her with him? "But what...why?"

"All very good questions," he agreed, pushing people out of the way as he tugged her along. "But I suggest we find someplace else to discuss them."

"I don't want to discuss anything!" she cried. "And why are we running?" she demanded. She tried to yank her hand free, but he held her wrist in an ironclad grip.

"Because I have an inordinate desire to see my next birthday, as, I trust, do you."

"What?" He was talking too fast for her.

He propelled her toward the nearest street exit.

"In case you didn't notice, you knocked a gun out of that man's hand. By the way, did I thank you?" he asked suddenly as they emerged out of the subway and into the street.

"No," she said, panting, as she stumbled up the last step.

He kept her from falling without even breaking stride. "Thank you." The words were tossed over his shoulder as he continued running with her in tow. People gave them quick, quizzical looks as they forged a path for them through the street.

"You're welcome," she snapped. "Where the hell are you taking me?"

"To some place safer. Look, Sheera, you dealt yourself in."

"I didn't deal anything!" she cried. "Why were those two men waving a gun at you?"

He didn't even seem to hear her. Damien stopped running. He scanned the heavily trafficked area, then waved his attaché case overhead. He saw the blue sedan. Murphy. Thank God he could count on some things.

"Over here!" he shouted and began making a path toward the car. Horns blared, but he didn't even notice. What he was aware of was the tugging on his hand in resistance. He looked over his shoulder. The woman was still talking. "What?"

"The gun," Sheera said impatiently. "What were those two men—" She got no further.

"Right now, lady, all I'm interested in is saving my skin—and yours, since it's attached to mine for the moment." He reached the car. "Get in," he ordered, throwing open the door.

"I will not," Sheera cried defiantly. "Enough is enough. I just came to tell you that you had the wrong attaché case and—"

She didn't get to finish her sentence. Damien had forcibly pushed her into the car from behind, then got in himself.

Sheera tumbled in. Pulling herself upright, she glared at him. "I was wrong. You don't have any manners. Just who do you think you're pushing around here?" She realized that he was staring at her legs. Angrily she yanked her skirt down.

He grinned appreciatively. "A lady who, unless I miss my guess, would like to stay alive."

His words made her gulp silently before she retrieved her courage. She did her best to glare at him. "If you think you're frightening me—"

He gave her a quick, silencing look. "I don't know about you, Sheera O'Malley, but I sure as hell am frightening myself. Drive, Murph," he ordered the rather round little man in the front seat.

He didn't look frightened, she thought as she assessed her Good Samaritan, now turned abductor. He looked exhilarated. "Let me out of here!" she demanded, totally bewildered and confused.

Neither man paid any attention to her, as if she weren't even there.

But she was.

Chapter Three

Sheera lunged for the door. As she swung it open and tried to flee, Damien pulled her back in.

"I'll scream for help if you don't let me out!" Sheera threatened. He held on to her wrist tightly. Desperation was beginning to set in. What had she let herself in for?

The blue eyes stared at her, an incredulous look creasing his brow. Was she serious? Scream? In New York? Who'd notice? He moved impatiently forward, still holding her wrist. "C'mon, Murph, can't you go any faster?"

"This is a BMW, not a tank. I can't plow through that." He waved a hand at the traffic in front of them. "Every cabbie in New York is out on Sixth Avenue this morning."

"Fine, they can each take a piece of us back to headquarters once those agents catch up," Damien muttered. "Turn up Fifty-third," he instructed.

Traffic there was just as bad.

Sheera's eyes grew wide. This was starting to sound like a bad spy drama. And yet, it was happening. Right now, to her. She shivered.

Code Name: Love

Damien felt her involuntary reaction and realized that if she *had* blundered into all this by some chance, she was probably frightened, frightened as hell. He gave her a quick, encouraging smile. It was all the time he could spare. The KGB agents behind them took up all of his attention.

He was smiling. There were two hulking thugs about to turn them all into confetti and he was smiling. What kind of a crazy person was he?

A crazy person who was kidnapping her, that's what kind of a crazy person he was. She gulped silently. This wasn't happening to her; it couldn't be. Where were the police when you needed them? *Be calm, Sheera, it's your only hope.*

It was hard, she discovered, to be calm when you were being kidnapped. The best she could do was to keep from trembling outwardly. Inside, she felt like a serving of Jell-O that had just been shaken free of its mold.

Damien craned his neck, looking out the window behind him. He could see the two KGB agents running up the block. For all their size, they moved swiftly, and they were catching up.

"Damn it, Murph, they're gaining on us!" Damien cried.

"Unless they've equipped this thing with wings, there's nothing I can do."

Murph sounded even more frustrated than her kidnapper, Sheera thought.

Thoughts quickly repositioned themselves in Damien's head. "Well, maybe there's something we can do."

Sheera had a terrible premonition that she was included in that "we." Sure enough, Damien reached over and opened the door next to her, pushing her out.

"We'll meet later," Damien told the driver as he followed Sheera out the door on the driver's side, away from the two swiftly approaching agents and into the middle of traffic. Maybe, with luck, if they wove in and out of the traffic, the men wouldn't see them, he thought.

He nearly tripped when Sheera refused to budge. "C'mon," he ordered, grabbing his attaché case.

"No," she cried adamantly, determined to stay her ground.

"Yes," he snapped back.

To her horror, he began to run, still holding on to her. There was nothing she could do except run with him.

Horns punctuated their zigzag path, blasting at them indignantly for daring to run between the cars and for moving faster than they were able to. Any hope Damien had of sneaking away went up in smoke. He looked over his shoulder and saw one agent pointing toward them. Actually, he could have expected little else. He was too well acquainted with the agents' dossiers to think that they would give up easily.

The woman was trying to pull away, and he gave her wrist a sharp yank. "This is for your own good, Sheera!" he yelled at her.

"Why don't I believe that?"

"You'd better." They were running toward the opposite sidewalk. "Those two guys back there never earned their Eagle Scout badges."

"And you did?" she retorted sarcastically.

"Head Eagle."

"So much for the Boy Scouts of America building character."

The conversation added to the unreality of the entire escapade. Maybe she was still back in Jackson Heights, dreaming. A nightmare like this would have been the perfect way to cap off the weekend she had endured.

No, her feet hurt too much. This was no nightmare. At least, not the kind you had with your head on the pillow. This was a real-life nightmare, the kind that made the papers every day.

She glared at the back of her kidnapper's dark head. The man had no regard for life or limb, she thought angrily as he dragged her behind him. At any moment, the traffic could come alive again. She had no false illusions about New York cabdrivers. They went over anything. Did he think he had a charmed life, like a cat? A cat—that was a good description for him. He moved with all the attributes ascribed to cats: quickness, agility, cunning. She had never trusted cats. She wondered if he had nine lives as well, and if he would lend her one. She had a feeling that hers was about to expire.

They had come to Eighth Avenue now and were still running. The agents had fallen behind, but one quick look told her that they hadn't lost them. They were still following.

They had left the prosperous atmosphere of Sixth Avenue behind them. Here, a few blocks away, was another world entirely, a world of derelicts and ladies of easy virtue. Dawn had sent the greater portion of the usual inhabitants back into the shadows, like owls, waiting for dusk again. But stragglers remained, hoping to scrounge a few more dollars. It was a world Sheera was unaccustomed to.

But then, she wasn't accustomed to being dragged along the city streets by a well-dressed maniac, either.

"Where are we going?" she demanded. The muscles in her legs were cramping up in protest, and her lungs began to ache sharply.

"You'll know when we get there."

He seemed annoyed with all her questions. *Well, let him be annoyed.* She hadn't asked for this. She vowed that if she got out of this alive, she'd never again even remotely flirt with anyone traveling the subway. In fact, she vowed to avoid the whole subway system entirely.

He darted across the street. *Didn't he see that red sports car,* she thought frantically as the driver jammed on the brakes for all he was worth. Obscenities filled the air as the driver leapt out. He looked as if he were going to run after them; then he changed his mind. Her kidnapper didn't even seem to notice.

"At this rate, we're going to have the entire city running after us!" she cried out, panting.

She had to stop. Everything within her was begging her to stop. She couldn't keep up this Olympic run any longer. "Damn it, let…go of me!" she demanded, trying to pull free again. It didn't work.

"I do, and they'll find you."

"It's better…than being run…into the ground," she retorted.

He gave her a very chilling look before turning back around. "They'd have a different end in mind for you."

The words were not said in any particularly menacing fashion. They didn't have to be. They carried a myriad of messages on their own, all frightening.

It was a bluff, she told herself. For all she knew, there wasn't anyone chasing after them anymore. It could all be a ruse. To what purpose she didn't know, but people didn't need reasons to do strange things.

She realized that she didn't want to risk the consequences if she were wrong. And even if she had wanted to, she still couldn't make him let go of her hand. She felt her strength quickly dissipating.

They dashed across Columbus Circle, scattering a flock of angry pigeons as they ran.

Oh, God, Sheera thought, he was heading for the park!

The situation was getting more serious by the moment. Once he had her in the park, she knew she'd be even more helpless than she was now. At least out here there were people, what little good that did. In Central Park, there were areas where no one would find her, especially at this hour of the morning.

"No!" The decree escaped out of bursting lungs. She tried to dig in her tottering heels. It was a totally futile effort.

He yanked harder. Damn her, what was wrong with the woman? Was she deranged, or just determined to die? It was her fault this was happening, anyway. If he hadn't been trying to figure out whether or not she was tailing him, he would have been aware of the two KGB agents before they had overtaken him. Then he could have merely led them astray the way the plan had called for. Damien was in no mood to be charitable. His only hope of losing the two agents was by running into the park.

He'd have gladly let her stay just where she was. But if he did, he knew what would happen to her. They'd find her and they wouldn't go easy on her. They would just assume she was working with him. But suppose she was just an innocent passerby? Leaving her would be tantamount to signing her death warrant. He was stuck with her for the time being.

He had had easier assignments. But then, easy wasn't what it was all about, was it?

"This way!" he ordered, pulling her into the park, off the sidewalk and into the grass.

On softer terrain, Sheera managed finally to dig her heels in. She felt them threatening to break at any second. "No, I am...not...taking another step. Shoot me...if you want to."

Damien stopped. The green light in her eyes challenged him to make good her statement. Still holding the attaché case in his hand, he cupped her chin and turned her head back toward the entrance. "I might want to, but they're the ones to do it."

The two men she had seen accompany him to the deserted store were lumbering through the park entrance. One held his hand under his jacket. Was he holding a gun? Sheera suddenly didn't want to see if her kidnapper's prediction would come true.

"Okay, let's...go!" she cried, falling into step as Damien began to run again.

This time, she offered no resistance. This time, her steps laboriously matched his, footfall for footfall. Sheera felt as if she were between the frying pan and the fire, and she had no idea which extreme this stranger represented.

"Look...if I'm going...to die...in...Central...Park, can I at least...know...your...name?" she said, panting, as they cut across a steep hill.

She had guts, he'd give her that, he thought grudgingly. A lot of women he knew would have dissolved into tears by now. Some men as well. "Damien."

"Damien...what?" she pressed, wishing she wasn't gasping like this. Thank God she had had the presence of mind to take up jogging. Otherwise, she would have been in a heap on the ground by now, twitching. And he'd probably still be dragging her along.

"Conrad."

It sounded like a name he'd made up on the spur of the moment. But at least she had a tag to hang on him, a tag that suited him, somehow. Damien was an unusual name, and he certainly was unusual. Not many men she knew had people with guns chasing after them.

Her thoughts were scattering in all directions at once, like a deck of cards thrown up in the air. *Satisfied? You're not bored anymore, are you,* her thoughts taunted her. No, no, she definitely wasn't bored anymore. "Bored" began to sound like a pretty good thing to be all of a sudden.

As they came to the crest of the hill, they passed two lovers who had chosen that very spot for its seclusion and were now utterly oblivious to the rest of the world. For a second, as she caught sight of them, Sheera envied them their passion. More than that, she envied them their position. Lying down. She wished she could. By now, she was on automatic pilot, despairing that she would never take in anything but a ragged breath again.

A blanket lay abandoned next to the lovers. To her surprise, Damien snatched it up with the hand that held the attaché case. It almost made him lose his balance. As he lurched, trying to regain his footing, Sheera stumbled next to him.

She looked at him accusingly as they began to run again. "What...do you want...with...that?" she gasped out. At that point, nothing would have surprised her—or so she thought.

She thought she heard him answer "Camouflage" but decided that she was mistaken. How could a blanket be...? Nothing made sense anymore. She felt as if she had been running all her life. Thoughts whizzed in and out of her brain. What was going to happen to her? Was the man who held on to her really crazy? Who were the men after him? After *them*, she corrected, a shiver splicing through her again.

And what was he going to do with that damn blanket?

She wished she had never looked his way. She wished she had never stayed with her sister, so that she would have never been at the Roosevelt Avenue station to look his way. This was what she got for being dissatisfied with a life that other women would have given their eyeteeth for. My God, she was a living morality play.

Sheera tried to stop thinking. Her mind was splintering, coming entirely unglued. She wasn't used to that. It unnerved her further.

"Here!"

She didn't know what "here" referred to. All she knew was that he had stopped running just as they were approaching a huge boulder. Sheera came to a halt next to him and then promptly collapsed on the ground.

It seemed to be exactly what he wanted her to do.

"Good."

"Good?" she echoed, opening her eyes. She was suddenly afraid of what was coming next. She began to scramble back to her feet, but he pushed her back down.

"No, stay down." And then he changed his mind. "Hold it." He lifted her upper body off the ground. "Get on top of this."

He was shoving the attaché case under her. If he meant it to be a pillow, he was certainly clumsy about it. He had it wedged under her shoulders, with her head dangling over the other side. She tried to remove it, but he wouldn't let her. Instead, he billowed the blanket over them and threw himself on top of her.

"Hey, now, wait just a minute!" she cried, becoming really alarmed. The length of his body covered hers, pressing her into the ground. She was instantly aware of every single contour. She was also instantly aware of the attaché case. It was digging into her spine.

"I'm sorry this isn't more comfortable for you."

The man was going to rape her and he was apologizing about the accommodations! Panic gripped her, and her hands flew up to claw at his face.

"Damn it, you are the most troublesome female I've ever met. I should have left you for them!" he grumbled, grabbing her hands and holding them over her head. She felt utterly helpless. "Now hold still!" he ordered in a harsh whisper.

"If you think I'm going to lie here docilely and let you attack me, you're—"

"Attack you?" he repeated, stunned. "Damn it, woman, I could very well be saving your life."

She had never heard it called that before. The best line she had heard to date was something uttered to her by a college freshman who had offered to "open the threshold of womanhood" for her.

"The hell you are." She tried to buck him off and was surprised that her body had any energy left at all.

"Stop fighting this or we're both dead!" he growled against her face. With both arms beneath her head, relieving her aching neck, he drew her mouth up to his and kissed her.

Sheera tried to twist her head away and his lips slid into her chin. "For God's sake, Sheera," he growled against her skin, "make this believable or you'll never live to kiss again."

He wasn't going to frighten her into submitting, she vowed. She kept her lips tightly sealed as he kissed her again. She continued struggling, surprised that his hands stayed where they were. If he was trying to attack her, shouldn't his hands be doing something? The fact that they weren't gave her some measure of relief. Maybe he was telling her the truth. Maybe this was just a ruse to throw off those men. At any rate, this was better than running.

Actually, it was a lot better than running, she thought as she slowly became less rigid. A warm, hazy feeling was filling her veins. She relaxed slightly, unclenching her hands. Might as well make the best of it, she told herself. If he *was* trying to save their lives, the very least she could do was cooperate.

There was a lot to be said for cooperation, she thought, parting her lips.

The two agents circled the area, paying no more attention to the two lovers than they had to the others they had just passed.

"Ci Amerykanie tylko myślą o kochaniu. Głupie kapitaliści," the larger of the two muttered.

"Ty lepiej myśl o swym zadaniu, Janie. Jak ja go znajdę, tego sukinsyna, to go rozerwię na kawałki."

The voices faded away as the two men ran on, still looking.

Damien was quick to roll off her. "They're gone," he announced, cautiously looking around. They were alone again. "Let's get out of here." He gave her a hand up and they were off in the opposite direction, back to the entrance to the park.

"They don't like you very much," Sheera commented as she resumed her place next to him.

"The feeling is mutual," he answered. He had caught a term that meant "son of a bitch," but beyond that, they had talked too fast for him to utilize his smattering of Polish. "Wish I knew what they were saying, though."

Sheera answered without thinking twice. "They made a disparaging remark about capitalistic morals and another about your parentage, and then the one with the deeper voice said he was going to tear you in pieces when he got his hands on you."

Damien came to such an abrupt stop that Sheera rammed into him. He stared at her. "You understood them?" he asked.

It had come so naturally, she hadn't given it a second thought. "Yes." For the first time since he had spirited her away, she smiled. She had succeeded in catching him off guard for a change.

He couldn't understand why she would foolishly tip her hand this way. With what had been transpiring, he was almost certain that she had been an innocent bystander. But not anymore. Well, he had her now and he'd take her to Bascom. Let her be Bascom's problem. Damien turned and continued to retrace his steps to the park's entrance.

"What's the matter?" she asked, confused. Why did he look so angry?

"How did you understand what they were saying?" he asked, pulling her down the hill.

Sheera tried to follow quickly. But down proved to be harder to negotiate than up, and she stumbled, sliding down the rest of the way. He tried to stop her, convinced that she was trying to escape. He wound up sliding with her down the newly mowed hill.

She found herself on his lap, a tangle of their arms and legs between them. She tried to recapture some of her dignity but failed. "I speak Polish," she snapped, pushing her hair out of her eyes.

"Why?" Damien wanted to know, pulling her up to her feet.

"Why not?" she snapped back. Honestly, he was the most exasperating man she had ever met. No one else had ever questioned her bilingual abilities. He had wanted to know what the two men were talking about and she had told him. What the hell was he being so annoyed about?

"You said your last name was O'Malley." It sounded like an accusation.

She couldn't see why he seemed so irritated. She tried to brush some of the leftover grass cuttings off her suit, but he didn't give her any time. Once again, she was trotting after him, held prisoner by his hand.

"It is," she insisted. "But my mother's was Kaminska. I'm half Polish—and all angry! Now are you going to tell me what this is all about, or do I—"

"Later," he answered, hurrying her along. The entrance was coming into view. He turned to look behind them. The two men weren't in sight...yet. "Your friends might be doubling back at any second."

"My friends?" she echoed. "I never saw them before. And I wish I had never seen you, either!"

Chapter Four

Sheera liked the Ambassador Hotel. Located across the street from Central Park, it was one of the older hotels in the city, standing regal and tall, with a wealth of stories sequestered within its walls. Stories of past generations, past majesty. She had walked by it countless times and was always struck by its presence. Whenever Starlight Cosmetics had important clients staying in New York, Sheera always directed her secretary to obtain accommodations for them at the Ambassador. Someday, she had promised herself, she'd spend a weekend there, just for fun.

Never in her wildest dreams did Sheera think she was going to be held prisoner there.

Yet here she was, being ushered into the hotel by a man who had become, in the past half hour, either her jailer or her protector, depending on which scenario she felt was more likely. And she didn't know which she chose to believe. Her feelings were bouncing back and forth like a tennis ball during a Wimbledon tournament.

The doorman, a huge man in bright, forest-green livery, grandly swept ahead of them and opened the front door, allowing them to pass. He gave them a small bow and a grand welcoming smile. For a moment,

Sheera entertained the idea of hurling herself at him and begging for asylum. He looked like a man who could protect her. He reminded her a great deal of her maternal grandfather.

But what if Damien had a gun? She had seen that the other men had guns and they impressed her as the types who would use them if necessary. But not Damien. No, not in the middle of Manhattan, she thought, rejecting the idea.

What made her believe that, she questioned. Maybe it was just that she was scared, confused and tired. Common sense sparred with growing panic. She no longer knew what to believe.

She felt confident that if she tried hard enough, she could pull away from him. But then, there were the other two men to worry about. And Damien had a "friend" who had popped up with a car. Maybe there were other "friends" scattered nearby. No telling what an escape on her part might lead to.

Whoa, Sheera. Get hold of yourself. That sort of thing doesn't happen in everyday life. Certainly not in her boring everyday life.

Her boring everyday life had taken a quantum jump.

She decided that the best action at the moment was to do nothing at all. "Where are you taking me?" she demanded in a low voice.

Damien was holding on to her upper arm now. The hold appeared loose enough to the casual, unobserving eye. Just a man and his companion strolling through the lobby. Only Sheera felt the warning pressure of his fingertips.

"To my room," he answered easily. His expression was purposely blank, unassuming. His calm tone intensified her anxiety.

"Why?" she challenged. What did he want with her? Actually, she really didn't think she wanted an answer to that question. Yet she was too straightforward a person not to demand one.

Damien guided her over to the elevator. Reaching across her, he pressed the button. As he did, his upper arm brushed against her chest. Sheera flinched and stepped back. He gave her a half-apologetic smile. But only half. "Don't worry, it's not what you think. I'm afraid, as inviting as the prospect might be, I haven't the time."

His smile unnerved her. It went right past her mounting panic to the very core of her being. What a time to think about being physically attracted, she thought disparagingly. "I don't know what to think," she retorted in a low whisper.

And she didn't. Was he kidnapping her? Could this all have something to do with Starlight's competition? Was that what this was all about? Sheera didn't fool herself. A lot of industrial spying went on every day. That would make some sort of sense out of all this, she supposed. But then she discarded the idea. She wasn't privy to any of Starlight's well-guarded secrets. Everything was actually in the hands of the chemists. She was in charge only of advertising layouts. No one would want to kidnap her. Her head began to ache.

"What I meant was that you're not in any danger from me," he told her.

She wasn't reassured in the slightest. "I'll be the judge of that."

She saw a slight grin form beneath the Van Dyke beard. "I have no designs on your virtue."

The elevator arrived. Behind them, a young bellboy and a woman of about fifty, wearing an outrageously long and obviously expensive fur stole, had joined them. The bellboy was struggling with an oversized suitcase.

Sheera hesitated. Damien gave her a helping nudge.

"And I suppose it's just your hobby to throw yourself on top of defenseless women?"

Her remark gained them a very haughty look from the woman swaddled in fur and a very interested one from the bellboy.

For a moment, Sheera again thought of screaming for help. But suppose those other two men appeared at any minute? She didn't know what to do. Those two men notwithstanding, maybe she would be better off on her own.

Damien saw the look in her eyes. He leaned his head forward, resting his hand on her shoulder. "Don't even think it." He whispered the warning into her ear.

His breath singed her cheek, and her face became flushed. Damn it. Did he read minds, too? Real fear began budding within her. She had made a mistake. She should never have come along so docilely.

The elevator doors retracted, folding themselves out of sight. They were on the fifth floor. Damien escorted her out. Sheera gave a backward glance toward the elevator. Just as the doors began to close again, she wrenched free and made a dash for them, much to the surprise of the elevator's occupants.

"Help, I'm being kidnapped!" she cried just as Damien's arm clamped around her waist.

The bellboy looked obviously confused as he pressed the button to hold the doors open. The woman in the fur stole looked decidedly annoyed at being kept from her destination.

"She's a little eccentric," Damien apologized, holding on to Sheera tightly.

She felt as if he were cutting off her air. "I am not!" Sheera struggled but it was useless. Proud of her agility, she was nonetheless no match for Damien.

"We had a lovers' quarrel." He winked at the bellboy. "She's trying to get even. My dad always said redheads had quick tempers," he confided in a conspiratorial tone. "C'mon, honey." He nuzzled her neck. Sheera jerked away from him, trying to ignore the strangely queasy sensation in the pit of her stomach. "Let's settle this in bed like we did the last time."

"There was no last time," Sheera cried desperately, looking at the bellboy for help.

"Sure there was." He held her tighter as he kissed her cheek. "That was when you bent into that strange position and—"

"I've heard quite enough!" the woman in the fur stole said in a huff, forcibly removing the bellboy's finger from the "hold" button.

Damien waited until the doors closed. "That was a very stupid thing to do," he chided her. His voice was low, but she could hear the controlled anger. "Now, will you walk or do I have to carry you?"

"I am not taking another step," Sheera told him defiantly. She congratulated herself on her bravery, but her self-satisfaction did not last long.

"Have it your own way."

To her surprise, he hoisted her over his shoulder as if he were a fireman. Sheera pounded on his back but to no avail. The man was a Neanderthal beast, even if he didn't outwardly fit the description.

He opened the door. The first thing he did was to put the attaché case on the desk. Then he deposited her rather unceremoniously on the sofa and went to lock the door.

Sheera jumped up, feeling better able to cope with the situation on her feet.

He put the hotel key in his pocket. "Now behave yourself and you won't get hurt," he advised. He gestured around the room. "Make yourself comfortable. Enjoy the view. I'll try to keep this as painless as possible."

It was a lovely suite, done entirely in blue and white. The decor was meant to be restful, but all Sheera felt was extreme agitation. Her mind raced off in a dozen different directions. Each path aborted abruptly, leading nowhere. She couldn't think straight. Her helplessness panicked her.

"Sit," he told her, nodding at the sofa.

Sheera glanced at it, set her mouth hard and remained standing.

"Okay, stand. Do whatever suits you." He shrugged.

"What would suit me would be: one, a complete explanation of what the hell is going on; and two, to get out of here and away from you," she snapped. Defiantly, she headed for the door.

He let her try the doorknob. She knew he had locked it, but she stubbornly felt the need to try. Her lock at home was always sticking and wouldn't catch properly. Why couldn't the hotel have the same kind of problems her apartment building did? She walked back to the sofa, glaring at him accusingly.

"All in good time, Sheera, all in good time." He looked at her for a long time, and Sheera felt as if she were being scrutinized from every possible angle. His deep, penetrating gaze made her feel as if his eyes were delving into her mind. "But first, I need some questions answered."

"*You* need some questions answered?" she echoed, amazed. "You're not the one who was jerked about, stuffed into a car, then dragged around the park and—"

Damien held up his hand. "I was there, remember? I don't need an instant replay. You will also recall that you were the one who followed me, not I you." He moved closer to her and Sheera backed up defensively. The wall brought an abrupt stop to her retreat. "Why were you following me?" His voice was suddenly cold, demanding.

Even with everything happening in kaleidoscopic fashion, she felt he was too close. Something about his presence cut off her air. It was just fear, she told herself. But she wasn't all that sure.

She didn't want to tell him. She felt like a foolish schoolgirl caught trailing after some unattainable dreamboat in the school hallway. "I wasn't following you."

"They didn't teach you to lie very well," he commented dryly. His tone became more demanding. "Why were you following me?" he pressed again.

Sheera lifted her chin like a prizefighter about to defend his title. "What are you talking about? *Who* should have taught me to lie?"

"You tell me."

Riddles. This whole thing was comprised of riddles. She wasn't going to get anywhere by hiding the truth. "All right, I was bored," she retorted.

Her answer threw him. "What?" he said.

Sheera looked past his head. She fixed her gaze on the flickering bits of sunlight that were being reflected from the chandelier and bouncing on the wall. Embarrassment colored her features, although she desperately tried to maintain her composure.

"I was bored. You looked interesting. I indulged in a whim." She turned her eyes back to him, angry that he had forced her to make this revelation. "Look, I don't see where..." She began to move away, but he gripped her shoulder and held her still.

"Do you often follow men on the subway?"

He wore a smile she couldn't quite fathom, but she could tell he was mocking her. He didn't believe her.

Sheera could feel her anger rising. "No, I usually stalk them in the steamroom at the Y," she spat out. "Look, I don't care if you believe me or not. I saw you and...and...I just decided to get off at your stop. Then I saw you exchange attaché cases—"

Her choice of words brought a fresh, alert look into his eyes. Sheera realized she had struck a nerve without knowing why. Damn, she'd have to be careful. If he thought she knew something, she might never come out of this thing alive. It had got to that, she thought sarcastically. She was beginning to think very melodramatically. It seemed to fit the occasion.

Sheera continued. "I just wanted to tell you that some man took your case by mistake. That was when I walked in on whatever it was I walked in on." Her tongue wrapped itself around the last sentence as the words tumbled out haphazardly.

"And you don't know either one of those men who were with me in the station?"

"No," she fairly shouted, getting tired of being interrogated.

His hold on her shoulder tightened. "But you do know Polish?"

"I already told you that."

"Tell me again."

"You certainly have a short attention span, don't you?" she shot back. "I won't answer you any faster with a crushed shoulder." She glared at his fingers. Gradually, he loosened his grip. "Thank you," she said icily. "I speak Polish," she repeated. "My mother was Polish. She was born in Warsaw. She married an Irishman. She wanted to have someone to speak with in her native tongue, so she taught me Polish. I spoke Polish before I spoke English. Satisfied?" she challenged.

He glared at her for a full minute, waiting for her to waver. She didn't. "Well," he said slowly, releasing her shoulder, "I suppose I believe you."

"Wonderful! Now I can die a happy woman," she muttered sarcastically. "Does that entitle me to go?"

"No."

A low, exasperated sound escaped her lips as Sheera began to pace about the room. "Those men have to be gone by now. It's safe to leave. And I'm already late for work." He made no move to unlock the door. "Why are you keeping me?"

"Does the word 'death' mean anything to you?" he asked.

Sheera froze in midstep. "Mine or yours?" she asked gamely.

She was certainly feisty. He found himself warming to her...cautiously. Playing with fire had its consequences.

"Yours."

"Why would they want to kill me?" She knew he had said this before, but it seemed so unreal to her. She just couldn't believe it.

"Because," he said very simply, "they probably think you're with me."

She thought she was going to scream in a fit of anger. *Steady, don't lose control now. All you have going for you are your wits.*

"Damned if I do and damned if I don't," she said helplessly.

Sheera assumed the bravest stance she could muster. She'd never had to do that before. Fear was not part of her life. She was always calm, controlled, in any given situation. But there had never been a situation to try her this way before. "Now what?" she demanded.

Damien was surprised at her tone. Well, she wasn't a coward, whatever else she was. Although her performance in the park had nearly convinced him of her affiliations, he still wasn't a hundred percent certain. He had to keep her around. If she was telling the truth, she was in danger. If she wasn't, he needed to know that. He also recognized that he wanted to know something about her. Something more than whose side she was on—if, indeed, she had chosen sides. He wanted her to be on the level. Why it mattered so much to him puzzled him.

Sheera wished that he'd stop staring at her like that. She felt as if her very bones were being examined. "What now?" she repeated.

"Now I make a phone call."

"Fine for you," she said irritably. "But I have a life to get on with." She looked at her watch. Five after nine. "I'm late already," she repeated.

"You're going to be later."

His comment frightened her and brought reality crashing down. This wasn't a bad dream that could end any second. This was real, with no end in sight. Sheera drew a deep breath. "Would it help if I gave you my name, rank and serial number?"

"It might."

"I wish you'd stop looking at me as if I just made the cover of *Spy Monthly*."

"Are you?"

"Am I what?"

"A spy."

Sheera's eyes grew wide at his ludicrous question. She hadn't meant her statement seriously. "Of course not!" she cried. She ran her hand through her hair, exasperated, her nails spearing strands. "Oh, come on, you can't be serious. This isn't some international plot I've stumbled into, is it?" She lowered her voice.

The smile he gave her cut through several layers of fear and created a very different kind of nervousness.

Spies?

Was *he* a spy? That would explain the switched attaché cases and the identical man, she supposed. And it would go a long way in explaining why those two men were looking for him. But, no, this didn't go on in everyday life. Not outside of Central Park. In the Ambassador Hotel. This was high drama for the outskirts of the Ukraine or some remote South American country that changed dictators daily.

She tried to approach the matter as sensibly as she would tackle any problem at one of her board meetings. Runaway emotions weren't going to do her any good here.

"Mr. Conrad, if that's who you are." *There, you're not the only one with doubts.* "I am Sheera Teresa O'Malley, vice-president of Starlight Cosmetics. Look, I have to get ready for a very important meeting this afternoon," she said, remembering the Donaldson account she was attempting to lure to her company. "Now I would appreciate it if—"

"Very convincing," he said with a nod of his head. "Especially the blazing eyes and flared nostrils—"

"My nostrils do *not* flare," she protested. The image made her think of a bull about to charge. That was definitely not the kind of image she had of herself, although she was beginning to feel as if he were waving a red flag in front of her.

"They flare," he said calmly. "Get into the bedroom," he ordered.

Did flaring nostrils turn him on? "I will *not*!" she cried.

He didn't bother to argue with her. Instead, he took hold of her arm and marshaled her into the next room. "Your virtue, as I said before, will stay intact. I have a phone call to make and I don't want to make it in front of you."

"Fine. Then I'll just be on my way and you can have all the privacy you want." She looked toward the locked door expectantly.

"Sheera, we've been through all that."

"And we didn't get to the right answer."

"The answer, for the time being and for your own safety, is still no. Don't look so downhearted," he said, laughing, as he raised her chin with his hand. "I've been told I'm a very charming person to be with."

She pulled her head away. "Who else vouches for you besides your mother?"

He patted her cheek. "Be a good girl and behave." With that, he shut the door behind her. He didn't want to have to worry about her trying to escape while he was on the phone. There was only one way out of the bedroom and he was in front of the door. He smiled to himself as he began to dial the number. If he was any judge of character, she'd probably try to listen in on the other phone. But he had seen to it that the phone in the bedroom had been effectively disconnected.

"Oh!" In a fit of frustration, Sheera hit the door with a clenched fist. Angry tears threatened to fall but she willed them away. She knew it was useless. She'd have to stay there until he decided to let her out.

Sheera wandered about the room, trying to organize her thoughts. She laced her fingers around the bedpost. It was a pleasant room. At least he had taste. He could have taken her to one of the flea-ridden, run-down hotels along Eighth Avenue.

Terrific. The man had kidnapped her, was going to keep her prisoner until God only knew when, and she was giving him points for taste. It wasn't happening to her—none of it—she insisted, as she walked over to the window. She was just hallucinating. Her mind had snapped because of her boredom, and— They were there, she realized as she looked down into the street. The two men from the park, from the subway. They were walking along the block as if they were patrolling it. They were still searching.

It wasn't a dream or a nightmare. It was real. Sheera backed away from the window, horrified. She sat down on the edge of the blue, gilded chaise longue and rubbed her neck. A tension headache was threatening to engulf her. What was she going to do? Was she with the good guys or the bad guys? And what was this whole thing about?

Her head snapped up as she heard the door open and Damien walked in. He couldn't see her from his vantage point. She seized her opportunity and darted behind him, trying to get to the door. He grabbed her, pushing her back into the room. "You've got to stop doing that," he warned, "or else I'm going to have to tie you up."

The very idea of being tied brought a bead of perspiration to the center of her spine. Sheera was claustrophobic. Being trapped in a huge hotel suite was hard enough for her to cope with, but being tied down would be unbearable.

"No, please don't." She hated to beg, but the dread his threat had aroused in her tinged her voice with fear.

Damien looked surprised. "That's the first thing I've heard you say in a civilized tone."

"Do all the other people you kidnap say 'please' and 'thank-you'?" she asked bitterly.

"I don't kidnap people."

"What makes me so lucky?"

He could see by the look on her face that she didn't believe him. "You left me no choice. If I had left you back there, they would have eliminated you." He made it sound as antiseptic as tossing away unwanted paper into a paper shredder.

"What do you intend to do with me?"

"I'm afraid I'll have to keep you for a while."

"What do you mean, keep me? I'm not a coin you just found on the street." Desperately, she grabbed his face and made him look at her. "Watch my lips. I don't know anything," she enunciated slowly.

"Perhaps not—"

"There's no 'perhaps' about it, damn it. It's not a crime to know Polish, or to be stupid and follow someone," she cried in frustration. "Why won't you believe me?"

He felt sorry for her. If she was telling the truth, this had to be a hellish experience for her. He put his arm around her in a comforting gesture. She felt soft and warm; her perfume wafted up to him. He shunted his arousal to the background for the time being. "My superiors think it best, for your own safety, if you stay here for the day."

"Just the day?" she asked suspiciously.

"And the night."

He felt her stiffen. "Your superiors can just take their opinions and stuff them. I have to get back to my office."

"You should have thought about that before you got involved," he said reprovingly.

"I didn't want to get involved! You dragged me into this!"

"Sheera, I have no intentions of arguing with you about this. Just accept it, and you'll save us all a lot of grief."

She crossed her arms in front of her. "All right, then what happens tomorrow?"

"We'll see."

She shut her eyes, struggling for control. Hysteria threatened to overcome her. "Very concise."

"Sorry, it's the best I can do at the moment."

There was a knock on the door, then an urgent tapping. She saw Damien become immediately alert, like a fox hearing the footfalls of an approaching predator. He took hold of her arm and his other hand slid into his coat pocket, poised tensely. She had been right—he did have a gun. Her breathing quickened.

"Who is it?" Damien asked, edging toward the door.

"Murphy. Is it all right to come in? I've got Cari with me. I had to sneak her up the back way."

Sheera looked at Damien, momentarily confused, but then reminded herself that she had somehow innocently blundered into a bunch of obviously crazy people.

Damien's hold on her arm relaxed just a smidgen as he drew his hand out of his jacket. "Come on in," he called out.

There was the sound of a key being turned in the lock and the man called Murphy fairly burst into the room, bringing with him the bag lady whom Sheera had seen at the Roosevelt Avenue station. Sheera half expected to see the White Rabbit run in after them, crying, "I'm late, I'm late."

"Everything okay?" Cari asked as she began to peel off the layers of tattered clothing, dropping them on the plush carpet.

"So far," Damien answered.

Sheera stared at Cari, recalling her fleeting impression of the jarring tidiness of the women's eyebrows. So, she wasn't a bag lady after all.

Cari stopped casting off her rags to look at Sheera. "What's she doing here?" Cari asked.

"She stumbled into a very cozy setup between me and those two KGB agents that Bascom had warned us about. I took her along for safekeeping. Bascom seems to think I should keep her."

He made her sound like a pet cocker spaniel, and Sheera bristled with resentment.

The three people in the room turned to look at her with suspicion, leaving no doubt in their expression that she was an unwanted intruder into their lives.

The feeling, Sheera thought, was mutual.

"Well, your Mr. Bascom's just made his first mistake," Sheera said haughtily, trying to sound brave. She hoped they couldn't hear the sound of her hammering heart.

Chapter Five

"What would you like to eat?" Damien asked Sheera as he began dialing room service. The others had come and gone, and they were alone again.

The bag lady had showered and changed, turning into a rather stunning brunette with the kind of figure that no doubt inspired appreciative comments from admiring men. She had taken the attaché case with her when she left, telling Damien that she was to meet with the all-important Bascom in half an hour.

Murphy had gone downstairs to the dining room for dinner.

The nervousness Sheera had felt just before Murphy's and Cari's arrival now returned to her, intensified, as she faced the prospect of being alone again with Damien. There had been something pleasantly reassuring about Murphy's moonlike face, even though he was one of "them," whoever "they" were. And the very presence of another woman had briefly restored Sheera's equanimity. She knew she was clutching at straws, but she needed something, anything, to help her make sense of the situation she had stumbled into. While Cari and Murphy were there, Sheera was able to take her mind off her own terror by trying to piece together the bits and fragments of information she was picking up from their conversation. Although they had kept their voices low, she had managed to overhear the words "scientist," "Poland" and "high-energy laser." None of it meant anything to her.

Now she was alone with Damien and it had grown dark outside. Somehow, the darkness seemed to make everything worse. Her thoughts were raging at fever pitch as she began to envision all sorts of dire consequences of her one act of whimsy.

"Well?" Damien asked, still waiting for her to answer.

"Nothing," she retorted. Her stomach rumbled quietly in protest. "Being held prisoner always makes me lose my appetite," she added sarcastically.

"You're not being held prisoner," he corrected her. "You're being detained for your own good. Now, you've already skipped lunch." Her stomach rumbled again, this time audibly. Damien grinned. "Why torture yourself? There's nothing to be gained by starving."

"I'm not the one torturing me." She glared at him coldly.

Damien placed the phone back in its cradle and moved toward her. He could see her stiffen. She was perched on the edge of the sofa, as if ready for flight. He sat on the arm and looked down at her. "Lady, you have no idea what torture is all about. I'm one of the good guys. I don't torture."

"If you're one of the good guys, I'd hate to meet one of the bad guys." She sounded a good deal braver than she felt, she thought.

"Yes, you would," he assured her quietly.

As he sat there, facing her, he remembered his first impression of her as she had walked down the subway stairs. He had been right. She was beautiful. There was something hypnotizing about her. He wondered if she knew how alluring she was. He doubted it. She didn't act like a woman who took advantage of her beauty for her own benefit. She hadn't tried to use her feminine charms to gain her freedom. If it weren't for the situation they were in, he'd have been strongly tempted to show her just how good one of the good guys could be. He had a hunch she was the type who could stir him to great heights. She had done so, too briefly, in the park.

That adventure in the park had been serious, but he had been in much worse predicaments. That was his job. He was trained to do his best under pressure. All his senses came awake at times like those.

And what his senses had also become vibrantly aware of at that moment was Sheera, beneath him on the ground. She had been soft and supple, and her lips had been warm and hypnotically tempting.

He was looking at her strangely, Sheera thought. An uneasy shiver ran down her spine. Was he contemplating what he was going to do with her? He had told her earlier that he was going to let her go in the morning, if all went well. But just what, exactly, did "well" mean? Well for whom? The statement had hardly created a sense of well-being in her.

"Who are you, Damien?" she asked suddenly, breaking into his train of thought.

"I already told you."

She shook her head. "You told me nothing," she corrected. "I know your name, or what you say is your name, but the fact is that there is another man running around New York who looks exactly like you. I also know that you can run like hell without getting winded. Not exactly much to go on."

He crossed his arms in front of him, studying her warily. Was she playing games with him? Was she what she seemed, or not? Headquarters was still checking on her. "And what would you like to have to go on?"

Sheera frowned impatiently. "You make conversation like a psychiatrist."

"Sorry...training." He slid down from the sofa arm and sat down next to her. Room service was temporarily forgotten as he continued to study her, trying to sort out his feelings about her.

Sheera moved away from him on the sofa. He definitely unsettled her, and the closer he got the worse her uneasiness became. She needed space to think. "What sort of training?" she pressed.

"Survival training," he said succinctly.

"And just what is it you're trying to survive?" She held up her hand to stop him from giving her another pat answer. "I swear, if you say 'life,' I'll scream."

She was one up on him and he laughed, enjoying a moment's respite. He put his hand on hers. "No more questions, all right?"

She shook her head. "No, it's not all right. I want to know what I've gotten myself into."

He hesitated for a moment. If she was innocent, she deserved to know something. And if she wasn't, what he had told her was something she already knew. "A ticklish international situation is about all I can tell you."

"International," she repeated. "That means you're not with the FBI."

"It could mean that, yes." He grinned broadly.

When he grinned he reminded her of a drawing she had once seen illustrating Milton's *Paradise Lost*, of Lucifer, beckoning. Lucifer, the most beautiful of God's angels before the fall.

Now what had made her remember that? This man was holding her against her will and she was comparing him to an angel. A fallen angel, she corrected herself. A living devil. She had to keep that in mind at all times. After all, Baby Face Nelson had been a killer.

She tried again. "CIA?"

Not a single muscle flinched on his face, but she thought she saw his brow move just a bit. Whether or not that meant anything, she had no idea, but she thought she'd push it. "You're with the CIA, then?"

His expression sobered. "It's enough for you to know that you're safe and won't be harmed."

"No, not really," she insisted. This whole affair was shrouded in mystery.

He cupped her face with the palm of his hand and caressed her cheek. "Well, I'm afraid it'll just have to do for now."

For some odd reason, she didn't pull away immediately. In that split second she felt a tingle of emotion swirl through her veins.

You're an odd creature, Sheera O'Malley, entertaining warm feelings toward the man who's holding you here against your will. Sheera momentarily muted her common sense, recalling what had intrigued her about him in the first place.

And that's what got you into this mess, remember?

She felt both anticipation and fear racing through her. For a moment, she thought he was going to kiss her. But she knew that could only lead to trouble at this point. She didn't know what or who he was, just that he was a mystery man who had two rather bloodthirsty agents after him. She thought they popped up only in international thrillers and Solzhenitsyn's books. She shivered.

"Cold?" he asked, realizing that he hadn't taken much care of her comforts.

"Someone's just walked on my grave," she said without thinking. It was an old saying she had learned from her grandfather.

"Let's hope not," Damien murmured, rising from the sofa. "So, will you eat?"

She was about to say no and then decided that there was no point to it, just as he'd said. He was going to hold on to her for as long as it served his purpose, whether or not she cooperated. She might as well eat; she would probably need her strength. Sheera nodded.

"That's better."

ROOM SERVICE brought a three-course meal that did not go unappreciated. Sheera had no idea how hungry she was until she started to eat. But her fork froze suddenly in midair when she glanced at Damien. He wasn't eating; he was just watching her. Why? She placed her fork down on the tray and looked at him expectantly.

"What's the matter?" he asked.

"Why aren't you eating?" she asked suspiciously. Was there something wrong with the food? It tasted all right, but... Her imagination began to run wild. Maybe the food was drugged. Or poisoned. It didn't make sense, of course, but then, nothing had made much sense since that morning.

She wondered if anyone was looking for her yet. No one would ever find her. There was no way to trace her. She simply had never arrived at her destination—that would be the police verdict. Another unsolved disappearance on the police blotter.

She was getting hysterical again, she told herself. But remaining calm in the present situation was difficult. She decided that, all things considered, she was actually behaving quite well.

She was almost transparent, he realized with a short laugh. No, she couldn't be a spy. She was just a poor, innocent bystander who had gotten in over her head. A poor, innocent, beautiful bystander with a way of hiding her fear behind a barbed tongue, he amended. He found himself admiring her for it. "I'm not hungry," he answered. "But I'll share some of your food, if it'll make you feel better."

"It would." There was no point in lying. Besides, if she dared him, maybe he would eat some of her meal and prove her suspicions wrong. She was still hungry and didn't want to let slip by the opportunity to eat if there was nothing wrong with the food.

He cut into her veal Scallopine and chewed the mouthful slowly, watching her all the while. He made Sheera think of the passionate eating scene from the movie *Tom Jones*.

For half the day her emotions had alternated between fear and rage. Now one small action from this nefarious man and her thoughts had jumped to sensual matters. Had she completely lost her mind? The answer to that, she thought, was probably yes. Otherwise, she wouldn't have followed him in the first place.

He took a forkful out of the center of her vegetables and took a sip of her coffee. "Satisfied?"

She half nodded. "Provided you don't have anything contagious." She eyed her plate.

He laughed. Her answer tickled him. He hadn't laughed for some time. "The doctor says I'm in perfect health."

"Nice to know," she murmured, scarcely paying attention to what he said.

"It is, for my mother."

Sheera's brows darted up in mock surprise. "You have a mother?"

"And a father." He grinned at her stab at sarcasm. "That's the way it usually starts, you know."

"After seeing that other man at the station, I thought perhaps you were cloned." She kept on eating, her eyes on her plate.

"I wish you hadn't seen that," he said with a sigh.

There she went again, sticking her foot in her mouth. What was the matter with her? Part of her success at Starlight was due to her verbal skills; she could always be counted on to say the right things to sooth ruffled feathers and to keep things moving smoothly. Why was she continually saying things to him that might put a noose around her neck—or, more likely, a gun to her head?

"A dozen people in the tunnel probably saw that," she interjected quickly.

"Yes, but none of them followed me."

"Not many Good Samaritans in New York City," she pointed out. Her dinner lay forgotten. "That was why I followed you," she said, suddenly thinking of it. It sounded innocent enough. Maybe she could parlay it into freedom.

"Why?" A dark brow arched quizzically.

It made him look appealing, she thought, momentarily forgetting the difficulty she was in. These mixed feelings were ridiculous. It must be hysteria. Handsome or not, she had to concentrate on getting herself out of there and away from him.

"Because you went out of your way and returned my wallet. You caught me by surprise and I didn't have a chance to say thank-you. When I saw that man take your attaché case by mistake, I wanted to return the favor. I had no idea that—" She stopped.

"That what?"

"That it would lead to all this," she lied. She was going to say "that the exchange was planned," but caught herself just in time. Let him think she was dumb. Dumb was much better than dead.

"All this will be over in the morning," he promised. "I know you don't believe me, but it really is for your own good. The department doesn't want innocent blood on its hands."

"What department?" she asked, trying to catch him off his guard.

He knew what she was up to. "My department."

He was impossible, she thought, disheartened. "What about tonight?"

"What about it?"

"Do I stay here?"

"Yes."

"With you?"

"Yes."

She didn't like the answer and bit her lip.

"Haven't I proved my gallantry yet?" he asked, amused. He knew exactly what she was thinking. And, he had to admit, the situation did tempt him. A great deal.

"Throwing yourself on top of me in Central Park didn't exactly give you the greatest character reference," she answered, saying the first thing that came to mind. Her thoughts had wandered back to that instance several times, replaying it in her mind, not only because of the fear and confusion it had engendered, but also because, she had to admit to herself, of the momentary sensations his nearness had aroused in her.

She pushed her plate away. He took her hand and drew her away from the table. "If I had wanted you, Miss Sheera O'Malley—"

"Ms." *Oh, God, now what,* she thought in panic, trying to sound brave.

"Ms," he corrected himself. "I could have taken you at any one of a number of times today." He reached over, his hands spanning her waist and his fingers dipping down to the top of her hips.

Despite her attempt to sound angry, she felt herself warming to his touch. Her mind grappled with her emotions to restore a look of indignation in her demeanor.

"I would have tilted your head, like this—" he moved her head back slowly, his fingers gently gliding along her throat "—and then I would have kissed you."

His lips were just a scant inch away from hers. She could feel her heart accelerate as she waited for contact.

Nothing happened.

"But I didn't." He smiled seductively as he released her.

He was teasing her, she thought. Somehow, he had sensed her reaction to him and had decided to have fun with her. Well, she'd show him that he didn't affect her in the slightest. "No, you didn't," she said in a low whisper, waiting for her voice to regain its normal tone. "I guess you were an Eagle Scout after all."

"My mother still has the badges."

A knock on the door interrupted their conversation.

Cautiously, Damien went to the door, his hand once again tucked inside his jacket. "Yes?"

"It's me."

The alert look faded from Damien's face as Murphy opened the door and stepped inside.

"All clear so far," Murphy assured him after flashing Sheera a smile. "I'm going to stake out the lobby for a while, just in case. You need anything?"

Yes, he needed something, Damien thought, glancing back at Sheera, but nothing he could allow himself to have. It would distract him totally. He shook his head. "We're fine."

Murphy had been with Damien since the latter had joined the organization. Murphy had taken the younger man under his wing to help him through the rough spots at the beginning and had seen him grow into one of the finest operatives the organization had. He was familiar with all the nuances in Damien's voice, and he detected something unusual there now. He looked from Damien to Sheera and then back again. "Yes," he said slowly, "I suppose you are, at that."

Now what had he meant by that, Damien wondered as he closed the door behind Murphy's retreating form.

Sheera sat tensely on the sofa, watching Damien. She cleared her throat. Their conversation was still unfinished. "What about sleeping arrangements?" she asked.

He turned his attention back to her. "What about them?"

"Who gets the bed?" she asked pointedly.

"You do."

That wasn't enough. He was clever at word games. "Without you?"

Her question surprised him. From someone else, he would have thought it was a coy invitation, but one look at the suppressed fear in her eyes told him that she wasn't being flirtatious. She was still afraid of him.

"Without me," he assured her.

She breathed a sigh of relief. Gratitude was evident in her face.

"See—" he spread out his hands as if to show himself off from all angles "—honorable all the way." Also slightly frustrated, he added silently. But his frustration would pass, and he was better off ignoring his desire. He had been around women long enough to know that she wasn't the type you got out of your system after one warm encounter. She made him think of a poppy—bright, attractive, with potentially addictive properties. No, he could do very nicely without that, he told himself.

"I'll just get a pillow and then you can have the room to yourself," he told her.

She couldn't hear what it was he murmured under his breath, but she smiled.

SHEERA LOOKED DOWN at her watch for the hundredth time. Were the hands on her wristwatch moving? It seemed like an eternity since she had left Damien in the living room, stretched out on the sofa, which was far more suitable for sitting than for sleeping. How long did it take for a secret agent to fall asleep? Did secret agents sleep? Or did they only catnap?

She sat, propped up in bed, tensely counting the minutes. It was ten-thirty. She had been in the bedroom for over three hours now. Three hours, ten minutes and fifty-seven seconds. No sounds had come from the other room for quite some time.

Had she gotten lucky?

She decided to chance it and ventured out into the living room. Carefully, she opened the bedroom door a crack at a time. She saw Damien lying on the sofa, one foot dangling down. He looked asleep. She crept closer. His breathing was soft, rhythmic. She waited, holding her breath. He went on sleeping.

Sheera crept by ever so slowly, tiptoeing to the door. He had probably locked it again after room service had cleared away their supper, but she couldn't recall him doing it. She was hoping against hope that he had slipped up. Slowly, she grasped the doorknob with her hand and tried to turn it, a fraction of an inch at a time.

"It's locked."

Sheera jumped and whirled around. "You're awake!" she said accusingly.

He sat up. "Obviously. I sleep very lightly. Occupational hazard."

Like a cat. The simile came back to her, as did her distrust for felines. She eyed him, her fears returning. "Are you really going to let me go in the morning?"

"I said that, didn't I?"

"You'll forgive me if I don't believe you," she said icily.

He grinned. "Have I ever lied to you?" he teased.

"Probably," she said as she walked back to the bedroom. She slammed the door in a huff. The sound of his laughter seeped into the room.

SHE DIDN'T KNOW when she fell asleep. Suddenly, she opened her eyes and it was daylight. She stirred. Her head throbbed. She had fallen asleep propped against the headboard. Her neck was stiff.

Water. She heard the sound of running water. Was that him? Was he taking a shower? She scrambled off the bed. This would be the perfect opportunity to go through his clothes and get the key.

Quickly, she made her way to the bathroom. Just as her hand was on the doorknob, the door swung open. Sheera fell forward, landing in a heap on the floor. She was looking down at his shoes.

"If you were that anxious to use the bathroom, all you had to do was knock," the bright, amused voice said to her.

"I'm not eager to use the bathroom," she muttered, embarrassed, as she rose to her feet. She tried to smooth down her wrinkled skirt.

"Oh, then were you eager to see me? Really, Sheera, I wouldn't have thought it of you. A Peeping Tom? Or is it a Peeping Tomasina?"

She raised her eyes defiantly, looking at him for the first time.

Except that, for an instant, she had no idea whom she was looking at. The man before her was dressed in blue jeans and a dark blue pullover. He was totally clean-shaven.

Sheera blinked, utterly confused.

Chapter Six

Sheera stared at the good-looking man standing in front of her. His slightly gaunt face, with prominent high cheekbones, gave him a decidedly sensual aura. Damien? Was this Damien? His eyes gave him away. Those crystal-blue eyes twinkled with that same amused expression he had had yesterday.

"Damien?" she asked, wondering what had brought about the transformation.

His laugh identified him beyond a shadow of a doubt. "Very sharp," he complimented her.

"Why did you shave off your beard?" she blurted out. She liked him better without the Van Dyke. He appeared less satanic. What a difference a little facial hair could make.

"Why?" Damien asked. He removed the last bit of shaving cream with his towel, then turned to hang the towel up. "Did you like my beard?" he asked.

"No." The denial came out a bit too quickly, she realized. "I mean," she continued, regaining her composure, "I never gave it any thought. I'm just curious as to what would make you suddenly shave off your beard. Oh!" The light dawned on her even as she asked the question.

"Oh?" he echoed, intrigued. He looked at her expectantly.

"You didn't shave it off on the spur of the moment," she guessed. "You'd grown it deliberately, didn't you, to look like the other man." She was quite pleased with her deductions. Especially when Damien nodded.

"As I said, very sharp." He took one last glance in the mirror. Satisfied, he turned to Sheera. "Care to join forces, Sheera O'Malley?" he asked lightly, walking out of the bathroom.

As she walked back into the bedroom ahead of him, she spied her reflection in the mirror that hung over the bureau, and frowned. She looked positively awful. Her hair looked like a windblown red cloud, bits and pieces standing up in different directions. Her clothes were rumpled and grass-stained. And there was that dark streak across the back of her skirt where the train had shut on it. All in all, she did *not* look like the capable, efficient vice-president of Starlight Cosmetics. She looked more like a "before" picture in a make-over advertisement.

Damien saw her frowning. *She's probably thinking she's a mess,* he mused. He thought that she looked rather appealing. He had lost most of his suspicions about her. Her attempts at escape had been inept, to say the least. If she were an agent and had wanted to escape, she would have been far more resourceful.

The key words here, he thought, were "wanted to." Maybe she didn't want to escape for some reason. He realized that there was still a little residue of lingering doubt in his mind.

When he had called his superior earlier that morning, Bascom had told him that, as far as could be determined, Sheera O'Malley was exactly who she said she was. That reassurance, plus the fact that the KGB agents had disappeared from the scene, gave him no reason to detain her any longer. Yet part of him was reluctant to let her go.

The job was far from finished, he reminded himself. He had no time to dwell on intriguing women.

"Do you still think I'm involved with the 'other side'?" Sheera asked, amazed at herself for actually saying that. The notion was too ridiculous for words.

But Damien wasn't laughing. Obviously, he took her question quite seriously.

"So far, the evidence seems to be to the contrary," he told her vaguely. His refusal to clear her totally irritated Sheera, but she said nothing. She didn't have to. Her eyes said it for her. His next statement made her forget her indignation. "My superior seems to think that you're out of danger. I'll take you back to your apartment whenever you're ready."

"Now," she answered eagerly. She dismissed the image in the mirror. She would take care of her appearance later. Right now, she wanted to take advantage of his offer before he changed his mind. "I'm ready now."

He nodded toward the bathroom. "Don't you want to freshen—"

"No. Nothing." She shook her head so emphatically that her hair bounced. "I want to leave now." She grabbed her purse. Within a moment, she was standing at the bedroom door, waiting.

He looked at her. There was a highly amused smile on his lips. "If I didn't know any better, I'd say you didn't like my company."

She was about to tell him that he was right, but something made her relent. "It's not you."

Why was she saying this? He had held her overnight against her will and she was concerned about hurting his feelings?

"I'm claustrophobic. I hate the idea of being trapped, of not being able to get out."

To her surprise, he seemed to empathize. Taking her arm, this time quite gently, he escorted her out the door. "I know what you mean. Get the same feeling myself sometimes."

She doubted anything as common as claustrophobia ever bothered him. He had sounded too exhilarated yesterday, almost as if he were enjoying himself. She had seen the expression on his face when they were running through the park. He seemed to thrive on danger. Some kind of derring-do in the name of God and country, camouflaging an Errol Flynn swashbuckling complex. She had already decided that he was some sort of government agent, and she was leery of agents, "theirs" or "ours." She wanted to get out of this whole setup.

"My address is—" she began as they stepped into the elevator.

"I already know where you live," he interrupted, fingering the keys to the car that Murphy had given him.

Sheera fell silent. Of course he'd know. There was probably a report floating around somewhere with her name on it. She wondered what else he knew about her. It made her feel very vulnerable, completely at his mercy. Was he really taking her home?

IT APPEARED HE WAS. The streets they passed were all familiar, she realized with relief, and then conflicting feelings again assailed her. Now that she knew she was going home, a sense of calm was returning, but it was an almost deadening sense of calm.

Damn it, Sheera, what is it you want? For the past twenty-four hours, all you could think of was escaping. Now that he's actually taking you home voluntarily, you're facing the prospect with dread. You wanted excitement and you've had it, more than you could handle. Now go on with your life.

She frowned as they stopped at a light. She had had that Donaldson presentation to make yesterday afternoon, and Haskell probably had messed it up. It would take her days to straighten it out. Back to fighting paper, smoothing out tempests in teapots and worrying about next year's line of cosmetics. Not very earthshaking.

"I thought you'd be more excited about going home," Damien commented. The light changed and he turned down the next street. "You've been frowning for ten minutes."

"Just thinking about what a mess my associate probably made of yesterday's meeting," she said quickly. "The meeting you made me miss."

"Couldn't be helped," he answered mildly. "Better to miss a meeting than the rest of your life."

The thought had a surrealistic quality to it. "Was I really in danger?" It was almost a rhetorical question. By now, she knew intellectually that she had been. But the thought was so alien to her that she wanted to hear him elaborate.

He thought she sounded intrigued with the idea. "Really," he answered. "You heard those men yourself—and understood them," he added, arching one well-sculpted brow. "Did they sound like the forgiving type?"

"No," she said slowly.

"And your timely entrance on the scene in that vacant store was what made them lose me," he pointed out. "For which I will forever be grateful."

She thought his words over for a moment as he approached Third Avenue. "Are you such a prize catch?" she asked.

He laughed. "In some circles. Certainly my attaché case was."

"But you exchanged it with that man."

He looked at her for a moment. No harm in admitting what she already knew to be true. "Yes, I did."

"So they were really after him?"

He placed a quieting hand on her knee. The warmth she felt disrupted her line of thought. It generated a sensation that had nothing to do with what they were discussing. Despite everything, or maybe because of it, she was attracted to him. Very attracted to him.

"The less you explore any of this, the safer you'll be." He stopped the car in front of her apartment building. "We're here."

Sheera glanced out. The doorman was standing at his post before the elegant glass doors. "Yes, we're here," she echoed. Was that she, sounding so depressed? She turned and looked hesitantly at Damien. "Well, I won't say it hasn't been interesting, Damien..."

He smiled. "Perhaps not interesting enough."

The words were soft, sensual, and she knew exactly what he meant. For an instant, she was moved to kiss him good-bye. Kiss her captor. Or was it her protector? At any rate, she was never going to see him again, of that she was certain. A pang of sorrow rose up within her, filling her whole soul.

"I, um..." She stuck her hand out. "Thank you."

He took it in his own, his strong fingers encircling her delicate hand easily. "This is quite a turnaround from the scratching, fighting female back at the Ambassador."

"The female back at the Ambassador didn't know what to expect," she informed him. Then her voice softened. "Now that you're bringing me home, I realize that you were only doing what you thought was best for my safety."

"I kept telling you that."

"I didn't believe you," she answered honestly. She realized she was stalling. She didn't want to leave, didn't want to draw a close to their relationship. Why?

He cocked his head as he leaned his face toward her. "Doesn't this look like an honest face to you?"

He was still holding on to her hand. And maybe, just maybe, a little bit of her as well. "No." She shook her head. "Wouldn't trust it any farther than I could throw it."

"You're a treat, Sheera O'Malley," he said softly, amusement highlighting his face. And then he cupped her face in one hand, just as he had done before...and this time he kissed her.

Sheera realized that she had been hoping during the entire trip that he would kiss her. Childish, she thought, but she wanted it. One kiss before parting, a kiss to remember him by.

No, she amended, she had two. Two very different kisses to catalog and remember when things got to be too dull for her. Two kisses to recall and examine from all angles, like multiplaned prisms that captured light and turned it into magic. This last kiss was soft, gentle, stirring. He drew her into it, both emotionally and physically, as his lips pressed harder against hers, transcending polite barriers and igniting something deep within her.

Probably came with his training, she thought, under the heading of "What to do with lady spies to make them talk." It was far more effective than handcuffs. Exquisite torture was more like it. Made you lose your train of thought almost entirely....

A horn blasted through the swirling haze about her head, bringing her back to Third Avenue and the lean doorman who was eyeing the occupants of the blue BMW with uncertainty.

"You're blocking the entrance! Go do your necking someplace else." The gruff remark came from a moving-van driver. He eyed the space they were blocking. He couldn't park his van until they moved.

Sheera flushed. She was both embarrassed because of her momentary lapse of control and angered with the truck driver for having broken in on her one last moment with the fascinating stranger. So much for her travels into the land of adventure, she thought, getting out of the car.

"Thank you," she said again, looking at Damien as she shut the door.

"My pleasure," Damien murmured.

She turned away slowly. She could see that the doorman was trying not to look surprised at her disheveled appearance as he held the door open for her. "Have a nice weekend, Ms O'Malley?" he asked courteously.

"It was—" she paused, watching the BMW slip out of her life "—interesting."

The truck driver had swung out of his cab and was approaching the doorman. "Looked a hell of a lot more than that from where I was sitting."

Sheera turned her back on him and hurried through the glass doors.

IT WAS NINE-THIRTY. Twenty-four hours ago, she had been embroiled in a life-or-death situation. Now she was standing in her bedroom, supposedly refreshed after a hot shower, trying to decide what to wear to the office. Her dresses merged into a dull blur as she listlessly pushed aside one after another. Her mind kept returning to yesterday. And to this morning.

He was good-looking with the beard. He was even better-looking without it. And beardless or not, he was definitely the most exciting man she had ever encountered.

Donald Duck would have been exciting in that situation, she told herself sarcastically. *You thought you were fighting for your life. Things tend to look different then.* Lately, the most exciting thing she had done up till then was to choose the right shade of lipstick to feature in an advertising campaign.

Advertising. The Donaldson account. She had to hurry to the office. As it was, they were probably wondering what had happened to her. She was never out. She wondered if they had tried to locate her. They had probably called Judy. She remembered mentioning her weekend plans to her secretary. She'd better call Judy to set her mind at ease before she left.

Grabbing a light blue print wraparound dress that fastened with two small buttons at the waist, she slipped it on and turned her attention to the phone.

It took eight rings before Judy answered.

"Hello, Judy?"

A wail answered her before her sister could. "Kirby, stop throwing things at your sister!" Judy bellowed into the distance. Her voice rattled Sheera's teeth. "Sorry," Judy apologized. "Sheera?"

"Yes. I thought perhaps—"

"Look, Sheera, if you're calling about your dress," her sister's voice came in a harried rush, "I haven't had time to get it to the cleaner's yet. Kirby's been acting up and the car's on the blink again and—"

"No, I didn't call about the dress," Sheera said. Judy's overactive two-year-old had spilled his hot-fudge sundae all over Sheera's white dress during their outing to a local ice-cream parlor. The entire incident now seemed utterly insignificant.

"Oh, about your overnight case," Judy guessed.

"My overnight case?" Sheera repeated dumbly, her mind a blank.

"Yes, you left it here."

In her hurry to leave her sister's house, she had completely forgotten about it. *It would have come in handy this morning,* Sheera thought. The last image of her that Damien had had was as a rumpled female.

Last image? The man probably wouldn't recognize her if he passed her on the street. She was probably just one of a thousand faces he encountered during his busy life.

"And Kirby put the goldfish in there, so I'm afraid that—"

"What?" Sheera asked, drifting back into the conversation.

There was an impatient sigh in response. "I said, your overnight case still has to dry out. Kirby put the goldfish into it and then the cat got it. I tell you, the book says to get kids pets, but the author sure never met mine—"

And undoubtedly would never want to, Sheera added silently. "That's okay, Judy, don't worry about it. Any of it. I'll just pick up everything on my next time through." *When the kids have gone to college.*

Sheera heard another crash in the background. "Look, I'd love to chat with you, Sheera, but Kirby just— Not the TV!"

The phone went dead.

Well, Sheera thought, at least no one had worried Judy with her disappearance.

She replaced the phone and sighed. She'd just go to work and tell everyone that she had...what? Followed a man with a beard, lain enmeshed in a kiss with him in Central Park while foreign agents swarmed around them and then spent the night in the Ambassador Hotel with a secret agent sleeping on the sofa?

She'd tell them she had caught a twenty-four-hour virus and had been too ill to call in, she decided. No need to tell anyone what had really happened. She wasn't all that sure that they'd believe her anyway. She wasn't all that sure she believed it all herself, now that it was over.

"Over," she said aloud to herself. The word dripped with sadness as it hung in the air after she'd uttered it.

"And you're lucky to be alive, if what Damien said was true," she muttered.

The man's name brought a fresh wave of something akin to longing. Stop it. He probably had a secret-agent wife and little secret-agent children tucked away somewhere, nice and safe. There was no reason to let her imagination run away with her over him. She had spent the past twenty-four hours heaping silent curses on his head, alternately fearing and hating him. Now she was rid of him and out of a scary situation.

"Time to get on with it, Sheera. You've had your one brush with adventure." She looked at her reflection in the mirror. It looked infinitely better than what she had seen in the hotel. Her hair was brushed smooth, pulled back into a chignon. The dress she wore flattered her waist and brought a definite hint of femininity to complement the picture of confidence and competence she projected.

Yes, she looked a lot better now than she had in the hotel. Even her eyes looked different. She realized, suddenly, that they had once again become lackluster.

She dreaded walking through that door again in the Endicott Building, dreaded walking back into her sedate, predictable life.

Oh, no, don't start that again, she warned herself, taking a long white shawl from the closet and wrapping it about her shoulders. *That's what got you into the mess to begin with. Act your age.*

Squaring her shoulders, Ms Sheera O'Malley, business executive, the glow in her eyes extinguished, walked out the door, ready to take charge.

SHEERA TREATED HERSELF to a cab ride to work. It took longer than public transportation and was far more costly, but she thought she owed it to herself. She needed a few more minutes to reshuffle her thoughts one last time. It had been quite an adventure at that. She smiled, wondering what Damien was doing right now.

You should be wondering what Haskell is doing right now and what damage he's done that you're going to have to undo.

Layouts, she suddenly remembered. The layouts were due this afternoon for the new magazine campaign. She had just given her okay on the model on Friday. She had wanted to oversee the shoot.

Somehow, none of that seemed as important as it had last Friday.

Last Friday she hadn't been kissed by a spy.

She laughed softly to herself, only to get a rather wary look from the cabdriver, who had, mercifully, been silent during the trip. He pulled over to the curb. "This is it, lady," he announced.

Yes, this was it. Time to pick up the reins she had dropped and resume her responsibilities, she thought as she paid the man. She stepped out of the cab and turned to face the building, bracing herself.

The familiar sight of her surroundings should have been reassuring, but she was depressed before she even reached her floor. She thought again about going on a cruise. She really did need to get away and renew her lease on life, she told herself.

"Ms O'Malley, *where have you been*?" The piercing question greeted her as she walked through the door of her office. Her secretary, Velma, jumped to her feet as if she had just seen her resurrected from the dead. "Mr. Porter's been screaming for you."

"Mr. Porter would," Sheera murmured. As the president of Starlight, Mr. Porter did little else other than scream and heap responsibilities onto her shoulders.

"And I have all these messages for you." The diminutive brunette held up a raft of pink slips to emphasize her statement.

Sheera nodded and just kept walking straight to her inner office. "I'll get to them," she promised.

Nothing had changed. Somehow, she had almost expected that it would. Silly, she thought.

"Mr. Haskell asked me to buzz him as soon as you got in. He's been absolutely beside himself..."

An image of two weak-chinned, nervous men standing side by side floated through Sheera's mind. Two Haskells would have been more than the world could have taken. Certainly more than she could take.

"No, don't bother," Sheera said, depositing her purse in the bottom drawer of her desk. She slammed the drawer shut with her foot. "I'll go see him." Might as well jump in with both feet and see what the damage was. "And tell Mr. Porter that I'll be along as soon as I finish getting a report on the damage," she said cryptically. She picked up the Donaldson file from her desk and walked out again.

"Were you ill yesterday?" the mousy-looking secretary asked hesitantly. She had been with the company four years and in all that time she had never known Sheera to come in late, much less miss a day.

"I was," Sheera said, chosing her words whimsically, "indisposed."

She left Velma looking very confused as she stared after her.

Sheera marched down the hall, bracing herself for Haskell's whining voice. Whenever things began to go badly, Haskell's voice acted like a barometer. The greater the whine, the more critical the situation. She shivered, trying to put herself into the right frame of mind to put up with all this nonsense.

This nonsense pays the bills on your apartment, she reminded herself.

Someone fell into step behind her as she turned the corner, but she was in no mood to turn to offer even a cursory greeting. She was feeling more confined here than she had at the hotel.

"Please to keep walking until you get to elevator," a heavily accented voice instructed.

Sheera dropped the file she was holding and swung around.

One of the KGB agents from the park was standing behind her.

Chapter Seven

Sheera froze. For a split second she entertained the idea of pulling away and dashing down the hall. But the man appeared very nervous, which probably made him even more dangerous. She decided once again that discretion and calm were called for. Discretion she could manage. Calm was another story. Horror began coursing through her veins like hot lava.

"What are you doing here?" she heard a strange, choked voice ask before realizing that it was her own.

He seized her arm and ushered her along toward the elevator. "Please to look natural," he advised in a low whisper as they passed several people. "You do not want to involve innocent people."

"But *I'm* an innocent people," she protested. She had no idea where her strength was coming from. By all rights, her entire body should have turned to liquid. This man was going to kill her. She could see it in his frigid, expressionless eyes.

The thin, bloodless lips curled in a merciless smile. "I think perhaps not."

"But I am," she insisted. "I am."

It was as if she hadn't said anything at all. The man punched the "down" button on the elevator.

"Sheera!" A nondescript man turned the corner just as the elevator arrived. The agent hustled her inside as Haskell stared, dumbfounded. "Velma said you were in!" he called after them just as the doors shut. He was holding the folder she had dropped. Papers were sticking out every which way.

She hoped she had looked sufficiently frightened to make Haskell call the security guards on the ground floor. *Oh, please,* she prayed, *just this once, let him be bright enough to see past his own nose.*

When the express elevator opened again, Sheera glanced hopefully around. There were no guards. Haskell had remained true to form. She caught her breath as the man at her side marshaled her past the one lone guard who sat, nodding, at his desk before the bank of express elevators. She tried to catch the old man's eye.

"No."

The command was barked into her ear as something hard jabbed into her ribs, its sharp thrust dulled by the jacket between them.

Sheera bit the inside of her mouth and kept walking, not knowing exactly how she was managing to do so.

"This way." The man yanked on her arm as they walked out of the building.

Sheera's body felt icy as he propelled her toward a dark, ominous car waiting at the curb. People hurried by them in all directions.

Grab someone, she thought frantically. *Anyone. Maybe he won't be able to get his gun out in time to get a clear shot.* She knew she had to do something before he got her into that car. Once inside it, she wouldn't have a prayer.

Suddenly, she felt herself shoved hard from the side. The force of the blow separated her from her kidnapper. She tottered, trying to regain her balance, but was jerked around in the opposite direction. Her hair whipped into her face as she half ran, half stumbled, away from the KGB agent.

Who—?

"Damien!" The cry tore from her mouth, and she felt as if she were going to dissolve into a puddle of tears of relief right then and there.

"None other," he tossed glibly over his shoulder, holding tightly on to her hand.

"Not that I'm not grateful," she gasped as they barreled down the street, zigzagging to avoid colliding with several pedestrians, "but what are you doing here?"

"You did so well yesterday, I thought you might want to join me for another jog." He looked over his shoulder. The agent was nowhere in sight.

"Tell me the truth!" she yelled at him, her voice drowned out by the sound of a car backfiring. Sheera screamed.

"This way!" Damien ordered. They raced across the wide avenue to a car waiting on the other side. This time there was no traffic to impede their progress.

Sheera fell into the back seat of the BMW as the driver started up the car.

"I see you found her," Murphy said to Damien, who had piled in after Sheera, forcibly pushing her over. The car was already moving.

"He found me," Sheera gasped. Her lungs felt as if they were on fire. She definitely had to get into better shape, she thought. For a few seconds, as she sat slumped in the back seat, gulping in air, she stared at Damien. Never had any man looked so good to her.

Easy, before you hand out laurels. For all you know, he's the reason this is all happening.

"How did you just happen to be there?" she wanted to know, trying to straighten herself but giving up. She felt as if all her energy had been siphoned off.

"Just my basic Lone Ranger training."

"Another trip down the garden path." She sighed. "All right, Tonto," she said, addressing Murphy wearily, "do you want to tell me what's going on?"

"Actually, I was coming to get you," Damien said before Murphy could answer. "Bokowski just beat me to it."

"Bokowski!" she echoed in disbelief. This was all getting to be too much for her. Sheera looked nervously behind her. The dark car was nowhere in sight. But that didn't mean they weren't out there somewhere, she thought uneasily.

"They don't want a direct confrontation, but they're still out there," Damien said, reading her expression. He put his arm around her. She felt so drained that she just sank against the warm comfort he provided. Her head dropped on his shoulder.

"He was trying to kidnap me," she said incredulously.

"I know."

Her head jerked up. "How did you know?"

"How is irrelevant. But it was the reason I was coming back for you. Your life's in danger."

"Again," she muttered unhappily.

"Again," he confirmed.

Sheera let her head drop, numbed. She believed him this time. She had living proof. *Living*. Would *she* be allowed to go on living?

This was all becoming a hopeless muddle.

Damien tightened his arm around her, letting her remain silent. *What a shock all this has to be to her,* he thought. *Or is it?*

As he held her, he couldn't help wondering if, just perhaps, all this wasn't part of a plan. Stranger things had been known to happen. And, the department had found out, she did have an aunt in Warsaw. Sheera could easily have been blackmailed into playing her part in this escapade, or perhaps she had been a plant all along. He knew for a fact that there were scores of people planted here for years, expressly for use in the distant future—people with impeccable backgrounds to throw the agency off. But their instructions came from foreign voices, their allegiance was to foreign shores. Sheera could very well be one of them.

Then why did you ride to the rescue when you found out that they were after her, he asked himself. Because he believed her when she said she was innocent. Normally, he would have called it his instinct. But for annoying reasons of their own, his instincts were thrown out of kilter when he was around her.

She was stirring against him. He let his arm drop. "So what happens to me now?" she asked as they stopped in front of the Ambassador Hotel.

"We go back to the room," Damien said, taking her arm. She looked rather shaky.

"What happens to my life after that?" She was impatient with his method of giving out information in dribs and drabs. She liked to jump to the heart of the matter, to know everything straight out. He was exasperatingly secretive, perhaps because of his training, but she didn't give a damn about his training. It was *her* life that was in jeopardy and she needed to know what was going on.

"We'll see," he said. They walked through the busy lobby and to the elevator.

"You are infuriatingly closemouthed, you know that?" she said tartly.

"One of my best features," he replied.

"Not from where I'm standing."

"And just where are you standing?" He realized he had voiced his question aloud. He hadn't meant to.

"What?" Sheera stared at him, confused.

"Never mind," he muttered, annoyed with himself for this small lapse. It had never happened before. Being around her was definitely bad for his career.

The elevator arrived and the woman in the fur stole who had ridden up with them the day before walked out. Instantly, she recognized them both. A frozen glare came into her eyes. "Being kidnapped again?" she said coldly to Sheera as the pair stepped aside to let her pass.

"As a matter of fact, yes," Sheera couldn't resist saying.

The woman muttered something inaudible into her chins.

Sheera laughed as the doors closed.

"That's the first time I've heard you laugh," Damien commented.

She looked back at him. "In case you haven't noticed, I haven't had much to laugh about in the past twenty-four hours," she pointed out. "And I don't now," she added with a deep sigh.

The room was just the way she had left it. For the oddest reason, she felt more of a sense of homecoming here than she had when she had returned to the office. That was the last bit of convincing she needed. High salary or not, she was going to look for a new career just as soon as she was safe again.

"Hungry?" he asked.

It was rather early for lunch, but since she had been in too much of a hurry to have breakfast in her own apartment that morning, the dinner she'd had here the night before had been the last meal she'd had.

"Lunch would be nice," she agreed, "as long as information is the first course."

"What sort of information?"

"Everything you want to tell me and a few things you probably don't."

He didn't bother answering her and dialed room service instead.

"Quiche," Sheera said suddenly, coming to his side. "See if they have quiche on the menu." She realized she was acting awfully blasé for a woman who didn't know what her immediate future held. But then, maybe she didn't actually believe any of this was happening. That would explain the sudden calm she was experiencing. Yet her fingertips were tingling, as if something were about to happen.

Did it have to do with Damien, she wondered, wandering around the room as she covertly watched him. She waited until he had finished his call. "All right," she said as she sat down on the sofa, "you've taken care of the food, now how about the information?"

He had a chance to admire the legs that had first caught his attention in the subway station. Her dress, when she sat, hovered just above her knees. For a fraction of an instance he wondered what those legs would feel like, wrapped about him; what she would feel like, dressed in passion and nothing more. He kept his expression blank.

Damien joined her on the sofa. "What is it you want to know?" he asked casually.

"For openers, why is the KGB after me?"

He leaned back. "Apparently they think you're someone important."

"Me?" She almost choked on the word.

"You."

"Why would they think something like that?" Sheera cried, stunned.

"If we knew how their minds worked, we'd be ahead in this game."

Game. Her life was on the line and he was calling it a game. "You people play strange games," she muttered, beginning to feel distressed again. If they thought she was important, they wouldn't stop until they got her, would they? A shiver went up and down her spine, a cold, frightening shiver.

"It's what keeps this country free," Damien answered.

He sounded as placid as if they'd been talking about Monopoly, she thought resentfully. Was he really cold-blooded? Beneath those sensuous lips, was the man devoid of feelings, of a heart? Had she lost her mind, indulging in a fantasy about someone who could very well be nothing more than a programmed machine? No, she remembered the relieved way he had looked at her as he pulled her after him in front of the Endicott Building. He cared. Whether it was because she was a fellow human being, or because she was involved in his case, or because of something else, he cared.

"And what'll make me free?" she asked, her voice hollow.

"The successful resolution of my mission."

"I see," she said thoughtfully. But she didn't see. She didn't see anything at all. He hadn't told her anything, she thought, frustrated.

There was a knock on the door and a young voice called out, "Room service."

Damien took no chances. He approached the door in his usual cautious manner. Sheera thought that it must be awfully unsettling to be on your guard like that twenty-four hours a day. Still, it beat falling asleep over the Donaldson file, she thought cryptically.

Opening the door a crack, Damien saw that it really was room service, for once living up to the hotel's boast of lightning-fast accommodation. He tipped the young boy who had brought their cart in and then they settled down to eat.

Sheera sat opposite him, but her appetite was not as keen as her curiosity. No, "curiosity" was too mild a word; that was a term one used to describe interest in the ending of a mystery novel. Her concern was far more intense.

"And just what *is* your mission?" she pressed. She saw the cautious look that entered his eyes. *Damn his training!* "I know you people are supposed to swallow cyanide capsules or something like that when someone asks you a question, but I think I've got the right to know. This is my life we're talking about. What have I blundered into?" she demanded, stabbing her fork at the quiche in front of her in frustration.

Ordinarily, he would have sidestepped her question with a barrage of double-talk. But his heart went out to her. He looked into her sea-green eyes, vaguely aware of their unconscious power over him. She deserved to know why her life was being turned upside down this way.

"All right," he said slowly.

"Thank God," she breathed in relief.

He suppressed a smile. "An important scientist was smuggled out of Poland last month."

"Who?"

"You don't need to know that," he replied, almost out of habit.

"Right," she muttered with a touch of sarcasm.

"He's asking for political asylum—as well as a lot of money." He said the last part with a trace of amusement.

Damien paused to eat a little of his steak. Sheera curbed her impulse to pull the plate away from him.

"He had been working on plans for a high-energy laser with two other scientists, both now mysteriously dead," Damien continued. "It seems that their government didn't want to take a chance on the plans leaking out in any fashion."

"So they killed the others? Just like that?" Horror rang in her voice.

Damien nodded. "Looks that way. The third scientist didn't want to join the ranks, so he managed to escape, bringing half the plans with him—the half that he had developed."

"Half?" She didn't see what good that would do. "Where's the other half?"

"Hidden somewhere in Poland." He watched her face for some sort of alert recognition. Her expression never changed. She was either very good or totally innocent.

"Do you know where?"

He weighed his words carefully. "No, not personally," he lied. Besides Bascom and the scientist himself, he was the only other man who *did* know.

"Then what...?"

"Seems the man doesn't trust us any more than he trusted his own government."

Small wonder, she thought, recalling how she had been carried off by both sides in two days.

"He meant to keep the second half as his insurance policy that his demands would be met."

"Why don't you just make him tell you the second half?" Hadn't she heard that these government agencies had ways of making people talk?

Damien shook his head. "He's not that familiar with it. The other half was developed by the other two scientists."

"Now mysteriously dead," she echoed numbly.

"Now dead...or presumed to be," he said.

"Were the scientist's demands met?" Why did she have to keep pulling answers out of his throat? Why couldn't he just come out and tell her? The KGB had been after her, so he had to know that she wasn't one of them, if that uncertainty still lingered in his brain.

"Yes, they were," he answered simply. To the letter. "The location of the second half was concealed in that attaché case I had yesterday."

"The one that other man left?"

Damien nodded.

It was beginning to make a little sense. "Then that other man—"

"Was the scientist," Damien concluded for her.

She let her fork drop back into the quiche. None of it had reached her lips. "That's why you were dressed that way," she cried, excited. "You were a decoy. You were supposed to lead them off."

He nodded again.

"And they think that I'm—"

"The agent sent to rescue the scientist."

"Oh, God," she groaned. This was more than serious. This was dangerous. There were agents out there looking for her right now. The thought made her want to cling to Damien for comfort.

Steady, get hold of yourself. It can't be as bad as it seems.

But it could, she thought. She had heard enough stories from her grandfather about what the KGB was capable of. She had always thought they were highly embellished tales, told for the benefit of a young, impressionable girl who had hung on every word. But now they all came back to her. Now they didn't sound nearly so fanciful or implausible.

She felt her knees dissolving. "And what are you going to do?"

"About you?" he asked, misinterpreting her question. "You're being put in protective custody until I get back."

"Protective custody" —the synonym for which was "jail." "Where are you going?" she wanted to know.

"To Poland." He knew that the other side had surmised as much. By now, they knew that he hadn't been the scientist they were after, that the government had the man safe and sound where, it was hoped, he could never be reached. The department didn't kid itself, though. If their agents knew certain facts, the KGB knew also. Intelligence worked on the same levels, and informers abounded in both hemispheres.

"To get the second half?" Sheera asked.

"Yes."

The idea seemed ridiculous to her. "But you don't even speak Polish. Why would they send you?"

"Because I'm the best man for the job. And I've been briefed enough to get by." He didn't add that he had been chosen for his ability to recall every detail of things he had seen months ago. There was no need for her to know that he had a photographic memory. That was the department's ace in the hole.

"But you'll need someone to help you get around," she pointed out.

"That'll be taken care of."

She should have known that it was. These people were far more thorough than she could have imagined.

Sheera began to feel the walls closing in on her.

Chapter Eight

"What do you mean he's missing?" Damien exclaimed, gripping the phone receiver. His clenched fist was the only outward sign that indicated anything was wrong.

"I mean missing. As in not reporting in for two days. As in gone." Nathan Bascom's normally dispassionate voice had a tight edge to it. He was sitting in his downtown office, telling Damien about the newest unpleasant wrinkle in their operation.

"Two days?" Damien repeated.

"Two days."

It wasn't like Stan. Stanislaus Kopeczny had timing like a Swiss watch. If he had failed to report in, something was terribly wrong.

"So I have no contact in Warsaw," Damien concluded.

"None."

"Any more good news?" Damien asked, loosening his tie. Suddenly it felt too binding.

There was a pause. "Our scientist has disappeared."

This whole thing was threatening to blow up in their faces. "When?"

"Last night."

"Kidnapped?"

"We don't know. He told the agent guarding him he wanted to see some of the things New York was famous for. Next thing our man knew, he was gone."

Damien tried to digest what Bascom was saying. "Think they have him?"

"Possibly. He wasn't exactly the most trustworthy soul as far as our side was concerned, either. He might just have decided to escape us as well. But if they do have him, they're bound to find out the location of the second half of the plans."

Damien ran his hand through his hair, agitated. "Terrific."

"That's the word for it."

The dry comment didn't fool Damien. He knew Bascom was extremely concerned about this new development. The success of any operation depended on checkmating the opposition. Sometimes they won; sometimes they lost. Bascom didn't like to lose.

"Okay, who do we have on tap?" Damien asked, quickly re-forming the pieces of the puzzle in his mind. He was trying to envision a new scenario.

"To interpret?" There was a long pause. "You're not going to like this."

"Nobody?" Damien guessed in disbelief.

"You guessed it. Care to try for the sixty-four-thousand-dollar question?"

"How the hell am I going to go to Warsaw without an interpret—" He stopped short.

"Conrad, are you still there?" Bascom asked, getting concerned.

Yes, he was still there, Damien thought, staring at the closed bedroom door. "Hold on, I think I have a way out for us."

"O'Malley?" As always, Bascom was one step ahead of him. That's how he stayed head of the agency.

"O'Malley," Damien confirmed.

There was silence on the other end for a good five seconds. Damien knew that Bascom was mulling it over, considering it from all angles and thinking of all the possible consequences. He could picture the man, cradling his ever-present pipe, rocking in his swivel chair. He'd been privy to the scene countless times.

"All right," Bascom said. "Take her. Security can't find any overt connection between her and the KGB. Only thing still bothering them are the regular payments she's sending to Warsaw. Might just be to help support her aunt. But I don't need to tell you to—"

"Watch myself," Damien interjected.

"And only let her know what she needs to."

"No reason to do anything else," Damien agreed.

"It's settled, then." Bascom sounded pleased. "Murphy will be over with everything you need."

The line went dead.

Damien hung up the phone and looked at the bedroom door. "Phase two," he murmured under his breath. Phase two was convincing Sheera that she wanted to go. It wasn't going to be an easy matter. His conscience stung a little as he thought about it. He was pulling her farther into the vortex. But it couldn't be helped. They needed that document with the second half of the plans. And they had to find it *now*, before the KGB got to it. Of course he'd be there with her, to protect her.

He hoped that Stan would turn up before they reached Warsaw. But if for some reason he didn't, Damien knew he was going to need someone to translate the document once he secured it. There hadn't been enough time for him to come anywhere near mastering the difficult language. But then, the agency was counting on his photographic memory. And he had counted on Stanislaus's being there. Like it or not, he now needed Sheera.

The situation was not exactly odious, he thought with a smile. He had had stranger bedfellows. He grinned at his own Freudian slip. Well, what would be would be, but right now, he needed to convince Sheera that it was far preferable to come along with him than to sit and twiddle her thumbs in protective custody.

And he thought he knew just how to do it.

Her claustrophobia.

"Finished calling in?" she asked as he walked into the bedroom. There was a sarcastic edge in her voice. She knew she was being unreasonable, but she didn't like being left in the dark this way. She hated having the door shut on her every time he had to make a phone call. It made her uneasy. He and whoever he reported to were deciding her fate, and she had a right to know what was going on.

"For now," Damien said mildly. "Come on out," he said, gesturing.

Sheera walked out and went over to the window. She looked down enviously at the people walking about so freely.

Good, he thought. "Murphy should be here in a little while. He'll be taking you with him."

"To where?" she asked suspiciously.

"I'm afraid I can't tell you that," Damien answered, purposely looking away. "There won't be much for you to do," he said, choosing his words carefully, "but you'll be safe."

Sheera felt a tightening in her chest. "How long am I supposed to stay there?"

"I'm not sure." He gestured vaguely. "A week. Two. However long it takes."

"A week?" she cried.

"If not more."

He saw her nostrils dilate slightly. She was fighting it.

"I can't just sit around for two weeks doing nothing," she cried.

"You'll be provided with magazines, books. They'll have a television and all the comforts of home."

"Comforts? Only if home is Attica," Sheera said sarcastically.

"Can't be helped."

She whirled on him. "Yes, it can. Take me with you." Her voice lowered. "Please."

Sheera wondered which of them was more surprised by the words. But a sense of desperation goaded her on. She couldn't cope with the idea of being cooped up.

"Do you have any idea what you're asking?" he said, sounding as if he were going to turn her down.

"Yes," she answered firmly. "I'm asking you to take me to Warsaw with you—"

"I—"

"To come along and untangle my life." She finished on an insistent note.

He shook his head. "It's out of the question."

"Why?" she demanded. She knew why. At least, rationally, she knew why. But this whole thing had defied reason from the very first. In a reasonable world, she should be at her desk now, working. But she was here and would remain here or in some place like it for God only knew how long unless she could convince him or them or whomever to take her along.

"You're not part of the organization. You're inexperienced." He began ticking off the reasons on his fingers.

Sheera grabbed his hand, holding his fingers immobile before he could list another reason. "The KGB doesn't seem to think so."

"That still doesn't alter the fact—"

She didn't let him finish. "I'll sign up," she interjected quickly.

"It's not done that way."

She closed her eyes, wishing that when she opened them again, this whole situation would have faded away, including him. But she knew that this was real—very, very real.

"Yes, I know, I have to be screened. I have to fill out an avalanche of forms baring my soul and giving out my innermost secrets, saying whether or not I ever cheated on a test in school or if my grandmother was a horse thief."

He wanted to laugh. That was exactly the way he always felt about red tape. But he kept silent and let her talk.

Sheera opened her eyes again and Damien was struck by the eloquent plea in them. "Don't tell me about how things are done. This is all so totally unorthodox."

She was losing him. She could tell by the look on his face. There was a trace of pity there, but pity wasn't going to do it. He wasn't going to let her tag along because he felt sorry for her. She had to make him believe that she would be able to help.

Without realizing it, Sheera tightened her hold on his hand. "I can be an asset to you. I'm fluent in Polish. I can read and write it, too. And," she added triumphantly, "I have an aunt there. She could be our cover."

This was going better than he had hoped. He had thought it would take longer to get her to volunteer. He almost felt guilty about setting her up this way, but it couldn't be helped. If he'd have come right out and asked her to go, she might have refused—rightly so. It was a risky adventure.

He could be placing her life in jeopardy. For a moment, Damien wavered, his conscience getting the better of him. But he had no alternative, since he knew what was at stake. This was a war for supremacy, and the other side would surely race ahead. He knew that it was fairly reasonable to assume that the copy of the document was not the only one in existence. They probably had several sets. But Bascom had told him that the Polish scientists had apparently managed to engineer a breakthrough of monumental proportions that could put the Soviet bloc considerably ahead of the Western world in military technology and quite possibly threaten world safety. *We desperately need those documents,* he thought with resignation. He went on listening to her anxious entreaty.

What was she doing, she thought in a lucid moment. She was actually pleading to go into the heart of a communist country as a spy. People got killed for that, didn't they? *If they got caught. So what makes you think you're invincible?* Damien had saved her before—twice; he could do it again. She put aside the unnerving thought and concentrated instead on convincing him. *I'll worry about the rest of it later.*

She interpreted his silence as hesitation on his part and went on talking quickly, jumbled thoughts falling together as she talked. "We could pretend that...that we were coming for my aunt's blessing."

"Blessing?" he echoed.

"Yes." Her voice began to rise as the idea took shape in her mind. "We could tell her that we'd just gotten married. That's it—married, and we wanted her blessing. How about it?" Her eyes shone with enthusiasm.

She looked so pleased with herself that he began to feel guilty again. He knew he should end the charade, but he didn't want the outcome to seem too easy.

For a moment, she thought she had him. But then he shook his head again. "Too dangerous," he said.

Sheera's shoulders slumped as her elation ebbed away. "So I'm to stay in protective custody?" she asked in an almost toneless voice.

"Yes," Damien replied and was startled by the incredibly haunted look that clouded her eyes. He crossed the room to her. "It won't be so bad," he consoled her. "Think of it as an extended vacation."

The hell I will, she thought, rallying. She gripped his arm for attention. "I can't just disappear indefinitely," she insisted.

"Would you rather disappear definitely?" he asked, but allowed his tone to soften. "What is it?" he asked, smiling at her. "A need for adventure, or has my fatal charm finally gotten to you?"

He was patronizing her and she didn't like it. "Neither," Sheera answered. *Was* it neither? Not really. Beyond her claustrophobia, an excitement bubbled. The prospect of traveling with him and being involved in an adventure electrified her. But she wasn't about to tell him that, because she surmised that that was exactly what he wanted to hear, what he *expected* to hear.

"I need to set my life back on track again," Sheera said after a while. "I don't like sitting on the sidelines."

That was what he had counted on.

YOUR
DREAMS
CAN
COME
TRUE
H·A·R·L·E·Q·U·I·N
FIRST·CLASS
Sweepstakes
Enter and you can win a
♦ Rolls-Royce™ ♦ Trip to Paris ♦ Mink Coat

A FIRST CLASS OPPORTUNITY FOR YOU

HARLEQUIN FIRST·CLASS Sweepstakes

- ♦ **Grand Prize** – Rolls-Royce™ (or $100,000)
- ♦ **Second Prize** – A trip for two to Paris via The Concorde
- ♦ **Third Prize** – A Luxurious Mink Coat

The Romance can last forever... when you take advantage of this no cost special introductory offer.

4 "HARLEQUIN AMERICAN ROMANCES®" – FREE! Take four of the world's greatest love stories – FREE from Harlequin Reader Service®! Each of these novels is your free passport to bright new worlds of love, passion and foreign adventure!

But wait... there's *even more* to this great *free offer*...

HARLEQUIN TOTE BAG – FREE! Carry away your favourite romances in your elegant canvas Tote Bag. With a snap-top and double handles, your Tote Bag is valued at $6.99 – *but it's yours free with this offer!*

SPECIAL EXTRAS – FREE! You'll get our free newsletter, packed with news on your favourite writers, upcoming books, and more. Four times a year, you'll receive our members' magazine, Harlequin Romance Digest®!

MONEY-SAVING HOME DELIVERY! Join Harlequin Reader Service® and enjoy the convenience of previewing four new books every month, delivered right to your home. *Great savings* plus *total convenience* add up to a sweetheart of a deal for you.

BONUS MYSTERY GIFT! P.S. For a limited time only you will be eligible to receive a *mystery gift free!*

TO EXPERIENCE A WORLD OF ROMANCE.

How to Enter Sweepstakes & How to get 4 FREE BOOKS, A FREE TOTE BAG and A BONUS MYSTERY GIFT.

1. Check ONLY ONE OPTION BELOW.
2. Detach Official Entry Form and affix proper postage.
3. Mail Sweepstakes Entry Form before the deadline date in the rules.

OFFICIAL ENTRY FORM

H·A·R·L·E·Q·U·I·N
FIRST·CLASS
Sweepstakes

Check one:

☐ Yes. Enter me in the Harlequin First Class Sweepstakes and send me 4 FREE HARLEQUIN AMERICAN ROMANCE® novels plus a FREE Tote Bag and a BONUS Mystery Gift. Then send me 4 brand new HARLEQUIN AMERICAN ROMANCE® novels every month as they come off the presses. Bill me at the low price of $2.25 each (a savings of $0.25 off the retail price). There are no shipping, handling or other hidden charges. I understand that the 4 Free Books, Tote Bag and Mystery Gift are mine to keep with no obligation to buy.

☐ No. I don't want to receive the Four Free HARLEQUIN AMERICAN ROMANCE® novels, a Free Tote Bag and a Bonus Gift. However, I do wish to enter the sweepstakes. Please notify me if I win.

See back of book for official rules and regulations.
Detach, affix postage and mail Official Entry Form today!

154-CIA-NA3Z

FIRST NAME_____ LAST NAME_____
(Please Print)
ADDRESS_____ APT._____
CITY_____
PROV./STATE_____ POSTAL CODE/ZIP_____

"Subscription Offer limited to one per household and not valid to current Harlequin American Romance® subscribers. Prices subject to change."

ENTER THE H•A•R•L•E•Q•U•I•N
FIRST•CLASS *Sweepstakes*

Detach, Affix Postage and Mail Today!

Harlequin First Class Sweepstakes
P.O. Box 52010
Phoenix, AZ 85072-9987

HFCS1U

Put stamp here.
The Post Office
will not
deliver mail
without postage.

Desperation gnawed at Sheera. "Damien," she said in a small, anxious voice. She wasn't used to pleading, but her frustration was threatening to overcome her. "Damien, I know it sounds crazy, but I really can be a help," she reiterated. "Do you have a cover worked out?"

"No." He drew out the word reluctantly, covertly watching her face. Triumph lit up her features, just as he had foreseen.

Sheera seized her opportunity. "Well, then, does my idea sound so bad?" She searched his face for some sign of acquiescence, but he was impassive. She felt a rush of impatience. Why was he resisting her so much? Was it because he still didn't trust her?

"If you're afraid that I might want to steal the plans myself," she told him, "you don't have to let me know where the document's hidden. I don't even want to know where it's hidden," she lied emphatically. "The less I know, the less danger there'll be of my letting something slip. Although—" she drew herself up slightly, her voice growing stronger "—I've never in my whole life let anything slip out. You don't get to be vice-president of a reputable cosmetics company by talking too much." It was hardly an apt comparison, but it was all she had to offer.

An amused look crept into Damien's eyes and it angered her.

"We have our own problems with spies," she snapped defensively. "The fate of the world might not depend on what new cosmetic formula hits the market first, but there's a lot of money riding on it. And money makes people do strange, dishonorable things."

"If you're trying to equate stealing a shade of lipstick to—"

"No, I'm not," she retorted. Yelling at the man was not the way to win him over, she warned herself. "What I'm trying to point out," she said, lowering her voice, "is a comparable level of professionalism. I'm as competent in my sphere as you are in yours."

"What does that have to do with anything? We're not shipping Avon ladies into Warsaw." *Careful, Conrad, don't overdo it,* he warned himself.

The tension she had been under since yesterday morning suddenly exploded. "You are insufferable, do you know that?" She began to pace the room. "They've programmed you into behaving like some sort of a machine. An android! You don't see what any of this is about, do you? You play with people's lives as if they were chess pieces, and expect them to fit into the roles you've assigned them. Well, I'm not a pawn, or a chess piece to flip off the board after you've gained it. I don't want to sit around obediently waiting to find out if Damien Conrad, Superagent, has triumphed again, or to stay in a godforsaken holding tank because something has gone wrong and I'll have to wait until some other Superagent flies in and does the thing right. Now either let me go back to work or use me!"

Her eyes flashed angry green lights, and he thought he'd never seen a more beautiful sight than Sheera O'Malley shouting at him. Something stirred within him, just as it had when he had first kissed her.

Sheera felt drained for a moment, shaken by the emotions that had poured out of her. She couldn't remember when she had last ridden an emotional roller coaster like this one. She stared at him, waiting for him to say something.

Damien only reached out and touched her face, in a soft, gentle gesture that seemed totally out of place with the upheaval of the moment. Then he forced himself to look away and said, "All right," using just the right degree of resignation in his voice, "I'll see what I can do."

Sheera sighed with relief. At least it was a first step. "Really?" Her voice was hoarse from her emotional explosion.

He smiled. "Really." He nodded toward the bedroom. "Do you mind?" he asked.

"Yes," she answered, "I mind, but I'll go." She walked into the other room.

She heard him close the door behind her. Her hands were knotted into tight fists; she had been clenching them throughout her tirade. Suddenly tired, she sank down on the bed, running her hand through her hair. Some of the pins loosened and her hair fell about her shoulders. Sheera pulled out the rest of the hairpins with annoyance and threw them on the bedspread. A glimmer of light caught her eye. The morning sun was shining into the room, its sparkle bouncing off the mirror. Sheera looked at her reflection absently. What she saw surprised her. She hardly looked like herself, she thought, touching her face in awe. The woman in the mirror looked like some wild-eyed, free-spirited gypsy. Light-years away from the cool, efficient Ms Sheera O'Malley. No wonder he was having doubts about her.

Alone with her thoughts, she realized that her own doubts had begun to surface. What had she been trying to talk herself into? Had she completely lost all reason? The project Damien was embarking on was dangerous, deadly—deadly, as in "dead." Although she enjoyed the heady feeling that suffused her when she felt that she was again in charge of her own life, she knew she shouldn't allow that feeling to propel her into a life-threatening situation. He was offering her asylum until this escapade was over; she was asking to accompany him on his dangerous journey. *Sheera, you're acting crazy.* But she knew that she desperately wanted to go with him.

IN THE OTHER ROOM of the suite, Damien reached for the phone and dialed a number. Within a few moments, pear-shaped tones were quoting the weather to him. He began carrying on a one-sided conversation with the recording, in case Sheera was listening at the door. He didn't like to deceive her in this way, he thought, surprised at the intensity of his reaction to her. She was one of the best-looking women he had ever encountered, but there was something more that attracted her to him, something in the proud tilt of her head, in the look in her eyes. One ought not to lie to such a dazzling woman.

Unless it was absolutely necessary, he amended, continuing to talk to the recording.

He'd make it all up to her when they got back, he promised himself. That allayed his conscience somewhat.

SHEERA JUMPED UP from the bed as Damien opened the door and entered the bedroom. She had been lying down staring at the ceiling and trying to pull her scattered thoughts together. Now, as she swung her legs to the floor, she looked closely at him, trying to discern what he had learned from his phone call. She felt a flutter of nerves in her stomach.

Damien stood silent, looking at her for a long time as he attempted to generate the proper mood. Finally he said, "Well, you won."

"I did?" she asked, stunned.

"My superior seems to agree that you'll be an asset, just as you said."

Sheera gave him an open, satisfied grin, and Damien winced as his conscience pricked him one last time.

"Glad to see someone in your organization has some brains," she quipped, drawing courage from her banter. She might be in need of more courage, but her nervousness was quickly giving way to excitement, and she wondered if that exhilaration was due to the prospect of her adventure or by the thought of sharing that adventure with Damien. Even as she had railed against him, even as she had reviled him for abducting her, she couldn't ignore the strong attraction she had felt toward him from the very first time she had set her eyes upon him.

Somewhere, somehow, he thought, looking at the radiant glow on her face, they were going to be lovers. He could feel it.

"So what made them see things my way?" she asked. Triumph and relief echoed in her voice.

"It wasn't so much seeing it your way as needing to see it your way." He came up to her. A tall, sculptured bedpost separated them. He circumvented it and curled his fingers around her waist.

Sheera felt a warm flush wash over her. She tried not to show it. "Come again?"

"You were right about what you said. I do need someone to translate for me. I've got a few languages to my credit, but Polish wasn't one I could pick up at a moment's notice," he confessed. He waited for a smug look to pass over her face, but it didn't. She was a rare woman. He went on. "The only available agent who isn't on a mission at the moment and isn't known to the other side is lying in a hospital in California."

Sheera sucked in her breath. "Bullet wounds?" she guessed, her voice slightly hushed.

"Appendicitis."

Sheera let out a long breath. "Oh."

"Nearly as fatal, though," he said, thinking of the time Murphy had undergone surgery. Murphy had been and still was overweight by some fifty pounds and the surgeons had had quite an assignment. It had been touch and go for a while.

"So I'm elected, then?" She was smiling openly now, the thought of bullets and danger briefly forgotten again.

"You're elected."

"When do we start?" She looked fairly ready to bounce out of the room.

"Whoa, not so fast." He took her arm and pulled her back to him. For a moment, he held her there, fitted against his chest. "We don't leave until tomorrow."

"Tomorrow?" she echoed, feeling her heart beating faster. "What do we do today?"

It was an invitation, he thought, one that he was more than willing to accept but knew he couldn't. Not if things were to go smoothly. He released her. "Today, we put down some ground rules," he told her. "I'm not about to put my life into your hands until you understand a few things."

His life in her hands. The phrase drove a new shaft of excitement through her.

Chapter Nine

The late-afternoon sun cast a rather somber shadow into the hotel suite. Damien had long since finished going over some basic instructions with Sheera. Satisfied that she understood her place in this scenario, he had turned on the television set. It had been either that or give in to the growing need he felt to hold her in his arms and make love to her. Television was an incredibly poor substitute, but it would have to do. Getting emotionally involved with Sheera might cloud his judgment, he feared, and that could cost them both their lives.

A noise crept into his consciousness before he became fully aware of it. He looked up to see her dialing the phone. In an instant he was beside her, his hand on top of hers. Gently, he forced her to place the receiver back in its cradle.

"What are you doing?" she cried, startled.

"What are *you* doing?" he countered.

"What do people usually do with telephones?" What was wrong with him? "I'm going to make a call."

"To whom?"

"I thought we were past that point," she said, exasperated. "I have to call my office. I can't just disappear without making some sort of excuse." She reached for the phone, but he pushed her hand down again.

"It's already been taken care of," he told her pleasantly.

She stared at him, dumbfounded. "But I—"

"Cari called in for you."

"Carrie?" she repeated. She didn't know any Carrie.

"The bag lady," he clarified. "She's good at impersonating voices."

"She must be a lot of fun at parties," Sheera said tartly.

"Your secretary thought she spoke to you," Damien added, watching her face. He knew she didn't like it, and he didn't blame her. He wouldn't have wanted someone to impersonate him without his knowledge. They were a lot alike, he and Sheera.

"And what did the bag lady tell my secretary?" Doubts as to the wisdom of her earlier decision assailed her. She was being drawn into a situation over which she'd have no control. And there was also the possibility of "accidental" death. Did she really want to get involved? She felt an intense fear grip her but, taking several deep breaths, she managed to regain her composure.

"That there was a death in the family and you were flying home to help with the funeral arrangements."

"I see," she said slowly. "And how long did I say I was going to be gone?" Might as well get as much information as she could, she thought, still feeling uneasy.

"About a week."

"Was I lying?"

"What?" He didn't understand.

"Is that how long it'll take?" Earlier that morning, he had indicated that it would take longer than a week. Had she caught him in a lie?

He paused. "We'll see."

"Your problem, Damien, is that you're far too definite about things," she said dryly. They had made a call for her by having some woman impersonate her on the phone. There was no need to do that unless they still didn't trust her.

She stole a covert glance at Damien. He was sitting in front of the TV again, as if nothing had happened. Unless *he* didn't trust her, she amended, putting it on a more personal level. "They" didn't mean anything to her. "They" had no faces, no names. He did.

Her emotions were vacillating between fear and anger as she stared at him. "Why don't you trust me?" she blurted out.

He inclined his head in her direction but kept his eyes on the set. A less perceptive person might have thought that he was still absorbed in the action on the screen, but Sheera wasn't fooled. "What makes you say that?" he finally said.

She stepped in front of the set, blocking his view of the screen. "Because I'm not an imbecile. We're going into an Eastern bloc country as a team, a team of spies." She tried not to pay attention to how ridiculous that sounded. "But you still don't trust me." She moistened her dry lips.

Sheera stood before Damien with feet wide apart, in an almost belligerent stance. Her hands were on her hips; her hair was flowing down her shoulders; her eyes were flashing. *A most provocative-looking lady,* he thought. Damien heard only part of what she was saying. He felt his desire for her heighten but kept his face impassive.

"That scares me more than anything," she finished, although she realized that the possibility of detection—and, yes, even death—should have been foremost in her mind. But for some reason, his lack of trust was even more upsetting.

Sheera noticed uneasily that he was staring at her intently; then her uneasiness gave way to an embarrassed pleasure when she became aware of the fact that he was looking at her appreciatively. For the first time she saw real emotion in his face, a palpable response to her, and she loved the sense of power she experienced.

Damien stood up and walked over to her. He attempted to place his hands on her shoulders, but she backed away. She knew she was physically attracted to him—had known that since their first encounter at the Roosevelt Avenue station—but she wasn't about to let him take advantage of her that easily. She was determined to control her relationship with him. "What you have to say you can say at a respectful distance," she told him, hiding the tremor in her voice.

He kept his tone mild. "All right. We didn't want you calling your secretary because we didn't want you to say something accidentally that might strike her as strange," he answered truthfully.

She truly wanted to believe him, but her expression betrayed her doubts. "If you're that afraid of what I might say accidentally, then my going with you to Poland could well be a monumental risk for you, couldn't it?"

"Maybe." He wished she'd stop probing.

Common sense told her to stop giving him any excuse for leaving her behind in some dismal cell, something she desperately wanted to avoid. But then, if he didn't trust her, why was he willing to take her along? It just didn't add up.

You're being too suspicious, she chided herself.

THEY HAD BEEN in the hotel room for seven hours, and Sheera was growing exceedingly restless.

Damien was calmly watching an old movie, *The Thin Man*, on television. The story barely filtered into Sheera's consciousness as she paced around the room, absorbed in her conflicting thoughts. Finally, she sat down next to him.

"He doesn't look so thin to me," she commented.

Damien looked up, slightly confused.

"William Powell," she elaborated, pointing to the figure on the black-and-white screen. "He doesn't look that thin. Oh, forget it," she muttered. "I was just trying to lighten the atmosphere." She looked at him. "You're not too quick for a spy, are you?"

"The title doesn't refer to him," Damien said easily, looking back at the screen. "It refers to a character in the mystery. And we prefer to be called agents."

I prefer to call you a bastard, she thought irritably. "You've seen this before?" she said aloud.

He grinned. "I could probably fill in the dialogue if we lost the voice on the set."

His answer surprised her and his grin beguiled her. "Old movie buff?"

"Old mystery buff," he corrected. "*The Maltese Falcon*, *The Hound of the Baskervilles*, *And Then There Were None*. You name it, I've seen all those corny old films. They're probably responsible for what I am today."

"Automated?" she quipped.

"No." He laughed. He liked her spirit. "An agent. As a kid, I loved mysteries, intrigues; loved the sense of danger that permeates those films. My father was a mailman. Dependable, solid. Never took a chance in his life." He smiled fondly. "I wanted something more exciting out of life."

She could almost see him as a boy, sitting in front of a set, watching in rapt attention as figures flickered across the late-night screen while his mother admonished him, unheard, to go to bed.

"What kind of a kid were you?" she asked. What went into creating a man like this, she wondered as she admired his handsome profile.

A commercial for a dish-washing detergent interrupted the movie, and Damien turned his full attention to Sheera. "The average kind," he replied.

She doubted that there was anything about him that was "average." If he'd been just average, he wouldn't have attracted her enough to have her follow him at the subway station. She had sensed immediately that there was something different about him, something special. It was evident in the way he carried himself and in those expressive eyes of his, so full of humor, zest—and caution, she reminded herself.

"Drove my mother and sisters crazy."

"No brothers?"

"None. I felt I had to be twice as much of a boy to compensate for the lack of support."

"Support?"

"I had two sisters who ganged up on me a lot."

"They probably had good cause," she guessed.

He grinned. He had the most engaging grin, she thought. It almost made her forget the jeopardy she was in, or that he was a spy.

"They probably did at that," he admitted. He felt himself in a talkative mood. Very dangerous in his line of work, he told himself. Maybe, when all this was behind them, he'd get a chance to tell her about himself, about the restlessness that drove him to leave his promising job at an advertising agency back in Los Angeles and try his hand at something that made his blood rush. He *wanted* to tell her. Odd. He examined the feeling for a moment before putting it aside.

The commercials came to an end and the movie resumed somewhat disjointedly, with no connection to what had happened before. Nick and Nora were now in an entirely different place.

"Looks like the film editor had a field day," Sheera commented. She stood up and started pacing again. She was nervous, restless, waiting for something to happen. She was a doer. She could never just sit placidly like Damien. But then, he probably had years of practice.

"I could fill in the missing portion for you," he offered.

"No, I haven't really been paying attention," she said vaguely. She had never learned how to relax properly, not since she had become involved in Starlight Cosmetics and had found herself on a constant treadmill. "This job of yours, it involves a lot of waiting, doesn't it?"

"That's to balance out the periods when there doesn't seem to be any time left at all." He got up and shut off the set. "It gets a little hectic at times."

"Hectic"—a nice, safe word to describe all sorts of unnerving episodes, she couldn't help thinking. He sure had a way of downplaying things.

"What are we waiting for?" she asked.

"Morning, mostly. And for certain arrangements to be made."

"Arrangements?"

"Arrangements." The single word hung in the air.

"Not exactly a fount of information, are you?" She ran her hand along the back of the sofa, lingering over the raised pattern of the brocade.

"If I were, I probably wouldn't be alive right now," he answered, approaching her from behind.

"Have you been in danger often?" she asked. Why this sudden desire to find out everything about him? Once this was over, they'd probably never see each other again. There'd be no need to.

She told herself she needed to know what kind of man he was, since she would have to rely on him entirely for the next few days. If things got dangerous, could she really count on him? Or was he the type to cut off ruthlessly anyone who no longer suited his purpose? She hoped not. But she had to be reassured. She turned around to face him.

"'Often' is a relative term," he was saying.

His vagueness grated on her nerves and she was about to tell him so, but as she opened her mouth, he took hold of her shoulders, and her words caught in her throat. Was he going to kiss her? She realized that she had stopped breathing in anticipation.

"What you need," he began softly, but then stopped.

"Yes?" Her voice came out in a low whisper.

He was about to say that they both needed to get out of that confining hotel for a while. But the suggestion faded from his mind as he held her so close to himself. Almost against his will—certainly against his better judgment—he bent his head toward her and kissed her.

Big mistake, his brain telegraphed. His body told his brain to go to hell.

Each time he kissed her, she tasted sweeter than before, sweeter and riper. He realized that he needed to possess her fully, and that his need was becoming an obsession with him as his physical senses struggled with his intellect. He stroked her back, fighting the urge to carry her off to the bedroom.

The force of his kiss had taken her breath away entirely. She felt an all-consuming fire envelop her yielding lips, and she found herself drawn to him like a moth to a flame. Later, she told herself, would be time enough to consider the consequences of getting burned, but right then, nothing took precedence over her overwhelming need to warm herself by his fire.

She was surprised and confused when he gently drew her away.

"What you need," he said, starting over again, "is to get out for a while."

She almost said "Oh," but caught herself in time. She didn't want her disappointment to be evident to him.

"You're getting cabin fever. C'mon, I'll take you to dinner."

"Where?" she asked dully, trying to hide her bewilderment.

He held open the door for her. "Don't you ever stop asking questions?" He sighed.

She shook her head. "No. I keep thinking that maybe I'll get lucky and you'll answer one."

"This is all very frustrating to you, isn't it?"

They walked out into the hall. Sheera noted that he had glanced around, ever so slightly, before he allowed her to venture out.

"Yes, it is," she acknowledged.

"Used to having all the cards on the table, are you?" He took her arm as he directed her down the long corridor to the elevator.

"For the most part. Unlike you, I hate mysteries. I hate having to wait for something to unravel. Simply put, I like knowing." She emphasized the last word.

"No surprises?"

"Only small, pleasant ones," she answered.

But then, she thought, as they walked into the elevator, if what she was saying was true why had she followed him to begin with? Because he had awakened in her a part of her that had been sublimated for so long, a carefree being who craved excitement. And he was the very personification of excitement.

He had been thoughtfully watching her during their descent. "D'you know something, Sheera O'Malley? I don't think I believe you. Furthermore, I don't think you believe yourself, either."

He was good, she thought. Sharp. "Do you make a habit of reading minds?" she asked as the elevator doors opened onto the ground floor.

"Absolutely essential in my line of work," he answered, only half teasing.

They were walking through the vast corridors of the hotel, passing small shops that were dousing their lights for the night.

Maybe he was better at reading her mind than she was at reading his, she thought. In that case, she had better not have any further thoughts about him.

But that wouldn't be easy.

ALLOWED TO JOIN the rest of humanity, Sheera enjoyed her dinner. The light buzz of the diners' melding conversations in the hotel restaurant added to her pleasure, and she felt exceedingly chipper.

She was not a bird to be kept in captivity, he thought, watching her. The dining-room lighting was dim, but it didn't hide the glow in her eyes and the radiance of her face. Not for the first time, his mind wandered to thoughts about her that had nothing whatsoever to do with the job they were about to undertake together.

She was frowning again.

"Is that an all-purpose frown, or is something else wrong?"

"I wanted dessert," she told him, ignoring his wisecrack, "but the waiter took away the menu and I can't recall—"

She got no further. To her surprise, he began to recite the dessert list—in precise order.

"How often do you come here?" she asked, not paying attention to the waiter he had summoned.

"This is my first time."

"Then how did you know...I mean..." She was having difficulty even forming the question. It seemed impossible for him to have memorized such an extensive list so instantaneously.

"Never ask a magician about his tricks," he replied with a wink.

He was a magician, all right. A sorcerer. And she had a feeling that before their association was over, she'd have a firsthand look into his bag of tricks.

DINNER WAS OVER much too soon, Sheera thought unhappily, lingering over her after-dinner drink as long as she could. She didn't want to go back to that confining room. Not yet.

"Time for Cinderella to go back to the kitchen?" she asked as he moved to help her out of her chair.

"Afraid so. You wouldn't want to be seen by the prince wearing rags, would you?"

"I don't know," she said, looking up into his eyes as she rose. She could smell the faintest whiff of his cologne. She had no idea that spies used cologne, she thought, amused. "Might be worth it. Might be an understanding prince." She was talking nonsense, but somehow she felt they were exchanging a message. Did he feel anything for her? The thought quickened her pulse. She knew *she* was attracted to him. Probably all that white wine with dinner, she mused, feeling slightly light-headed.

"He might turn out to be an understanding prince," Damien agreed, "but that's not how the story's written." He escorted her out. He nodded at someone.

Sheera automatically glanced in that direction. Murphy was just finishing up his meal, his round stomach pushed against the table. She smiled at him and waved.

"Or wasn't I supposed to do that?" she asked in a whisper, leaning her head toward Damien.

"Waving is allowed in this country. Try to curb it when we fly over the meridian," he quipped.

She wasn't sure if he was serious or only teasing. *Complicated man, this Damien Conrad.* She sighed.

The hotel labyrinth they entered led them past a corridor of ballrooms, all bearing the names of different gems. The more expensive the gem, the larger the room. Music was emanating from the Emerald Room, its doors open, as if in invitation.

Sheera stopped to look in. A party was in progress, and there were people dancing. Women in evening wear were gliding by with crisply dressed men, swaying to the music. Without realizing it, Sheera began to move to the sultry beat.

For a moment, Damien contented himself with watching the way her hips swayed. Then, moving behind her, he asked, "Want to dance?" There was no reason, he thought, why she shouldn't enjoy herself a little. After all, he had put her into this predicament, and he felt he owed her something.

Sheera smiled and nodded, still looking into the room. To her surprise, he took her hand and began to lead her in.

"Oh, but we can't," she whispered, reluctant. "We don't know these people."

"We don't have to," he answered in a beguiling conspiratorial tone.

"But—" The protest was halfhearted. She really did want to dance. "We can't just waltz in—"

"We won't. The band isn't playing a waltz."

"We don't fit in," she murmured, beginning to relent.

"I always fit in," he assured her. There was a momentary twinkle in his eye that she wasn't quite sure how to interpret.

"But—"

"Shh." He laid a finger to his lips and winked, then turned around and led her into the room, his manner indicating that they were merely a couple who had stepped out of the ballroom momentarily and were now returning.

"Pardon me...excuse me." They threaded their way through a cluster of people who were standing about with heaping plates of food in their hands. To one side stood a table with the remains of a towering wedding cake. The "bride and groom" in this case were a couple in their sixties who were celebrating the renewal of their vows along with their children and grandchildren and, it seemed, about half of Manhattan's total population.

Damien and Sheera stopped near the small band. In deference to the elderly couple's age, a medley of old songs was being played—wonderful, dreamy old songs. Damien took Sheera into his arms and held her close.

He curled her hand beneath his and pressed it against his chest. Sheera leaned her head against his shoulder, allowing herself to drift with the music. All this wasn't really happening, she thought. Here she was, crashing a party, dancing with a spy in a ballroom in the Ambassador Hotel.

Well, you were the one who wanted something different, she told herself. *And this certainly is something different.*

"Nice perfume."

The words cut into her thoughts. She lifted her head almost reluctantly, afraid to break the spell.

"What?" she murmured.

"Is that one of your products?"

She nodded. "Formula number 367." That sounded like something within his line. "Midnight Madness to the masses," she clarified.

"It fits," he whispered into her hair as she pressed her head to his shoulder again.

He was right, she thought. Was this a moment of peace preceding the start of the real madness?

Chapter Ten

"I think we'd better go."

Damien's voice came floating softly down to her ear. Sheera didn't want the evening to end. Wrapped in the haze of wine and music, she had allowed her feelings to flower. His rhythmic breathing was comforting to her, like the soothing sound to a newborn of its mother's heartbeat. She felt cocooned, safe—and very, very romantic.

Wouldn't he be surprised if he knew, she mused. Would his Superagent facade crack just a little? No, probably not. Anyway, he probably knew what she was thinking. He was probably probing her mind right now. For a second, she felt embarrassed.

She lifted her head. "So soon?" It wasn't what she had meant to say, but the protest escaped her lips before she was aware of it.

He smiled at her, a smile that seeped deep into her senses. *Wonderful stuff, wine,* she thought. *Puts a bright glow on everything.*

"We've been here almost two hours. The party's beginning to thin out. Someone just might realize that no one knows us."

She nodded. They stopped dancing and he took her hand, leading her out. She smiled at several of the couples they passed.

The air outside felt cooler than it had been in the ballroom. The density of people in the room must have overtaxed the air-conditioning system. The air had been hot, almost steamy.

Like her, she thought with a smile.

Now, with the rush of cooler air swirling about her, she felt like a swimmer bobbing her head out of warm water, the cold stinging her face, making her alert. Time to come back to reality. The reality was that she was with a secret agent who was affiliated with an agency whose name he wouldn't reveal. The reality was that he was very, very handsome.

She cleared her throat, hoping to clear her mind.

"Did you say something?" he asked as they approached the elevator.

She shook her head. "No, but I should have said thank-you."

"For what?" He looked surprised.

She nodded her head toward the ballroom. "For indulging me." He had been sensitive to her need, and she was grateful to him for that gesture.

He smiled. "I always try to accommodate beautiful women."

Probably in more ways than one, she thought. She loved his roguish smile. That's what it was about him that attracted her, that roguish, unpredictable style. He had an air of adventure about him. Why couldn't they just be on a date? Why couldn't she have met him at a tennis club instead of during his attempt to flee from the KGB?

That evening had shown her another side of him. Before, she had only seen him acting in his professional capacity. Now she had seen Damien the man. He was interesting, amusing, enticing, even sweet, and he hadn't lost that unpredictable, devilish quality of his.

"You really didn't have to do that, you know," she told him.

"I know. But I thought that I owed it to you after what I've put you through."

She wondered what else he thought he owed her. Nervous anticipation shot alternating hot and cold shivers through her.

They rode up in silence.

"Same arrangements tonight?" she asked as they entered the suite. She was almost tempting him into a closer relationship. She hadn't felt like this since... Never before, she realized. He made everything seem brand-new.

Damien was busy looking around the room, to make sure that nothing had been disturbed, and paying little attention to what she was saying. "What?"

"Sleeping arrangements," she clarified. "Same as last night? Or do I get the couch tonight?" *Or do you have something else in mind,* she added silently.

"No, no couch," he answered.

He drew her closer to him. The smell of her perfume while they were dancing had permeated his senses and heightened his desire for her.

"Chivalry dictates that I give you the bed again." He combed his fingers through her hair. It felt thick and rich, and he barely suppressed an urge to bury his face in it.

"I didn't know the Superagent code calls for chivalry," she said. The pulse in her throat was throbbing and all her senses were opening up to him. The room was a blur.

"We each write our own code as we go along," he told her. His eyes caressed her face softly. "There still is some individuality within this job." The words were slow, drawn out, but neither Sheera nor Damien were listening to the literal meaning. Their thoughts had reached a different level, where words were pushed aside by feelings.

His hands slipped from her hair down to her shoulders, then to her back as he took her into his arms. Sheera tilted her head, standing up on her toes to reach his kiss before it descended.

This time, it wasn't so gentle. This time, she felt, much to her own surprise and pleasure, that there was more emotion to it, more of a taste of desire. Damien's hold on her tightened as his body molded against hers. Sheera felt herself growing breathless as she absorbed the passion in his kiss and matched its intensity with her own.

A faint hint of wine still lingered on her lips, but she was intoxicating enough without it, he thought. Once again, the urge to lift her up in his arms and carry her into the bedroom swept over him, stronger than ever. He felt an overwhelming, irresistible ache for her.

But he knew he had to repress it. Although he had playfully told her that each agent wrote his own code, he held fast to one rule in his code: he never allowed himself to be distracted during a mission. And she was definitely a distraction. To make love to her in the way he wanted to would make him forget everything, he feared, for she was the kind of woman who would not leave one's system, stimulating the need rather than checking it. Wanting her could very well become a disease of the blood for him.

Ever so gently, he pulled her arms from around his neck. The bright sea-green eyes, hazed over with desire, blinked, then stared at him, uncomprehending. Why had he stopped?

"I think we'd both better get some sleep. Tomorrow isn't all that far off."

Tomorrow. Thoughts of tomorrow had been completely erased from her mind. All she cared about was tonight, this moment, about exploring the wondrous sensations he had aroused within her. Sheera searched his face and was satisfied to see that there was just a touch of longing in his eyes.

So, Secret Agent Man, you can feel, can't you?

She accepted his excuse with a slight nod of her head, hiding the forlorn pang of disappointment. "See you in the morning," she murmured.

Better this way, Sheera, me girl. Falling in love with a man who darts in and out of shadows for a living isn't the smartest thing you could do.

But then, she had never imagined that love was linked with being smart. Love was something that just happened to people, if they were lucky. It had never happened to her before.

Probably not happening now, either, she reflected as she shut the bedroom door behind her. *It's just the excitement, the magic of the moment and the wine.* If she had taken him to her bed tonight, tomorrow morning she would have awakened in horror over what she had done on impulse. Sheera never acted impulsively.

But she *had* followed him, she reminded herself, sinking down on her bed.

She felt something beneath her outstretched hand and looked down. A nightgown lay stretched out on the bed. Her nightgown. She stared at it as if it were a foreign object. When...?

"Damien," she called out, still looking at the lavender garment.

Her door opened in a flash. "What?" He scanned the room quickly, searching for whatever it was that had made her call out. Because of his momentary preoccupation with her, he had failed to check the adjacent room. That was why, he told himself pointedly, dalliances were strictly forbidden.

"What is this doing here?" she asked, holding up her nightgown.

It was a light, translucent thing and he couldn't help wondering what she looked like in it.

"Cari packed for you. You'll find the rest of your things in a suitcase in the closet. She dropped it off while we were at dinner."

Cari, the bag lady. The voice impersonator. "I'll also need my purse and a passport," she reminded him, trying to think logically.

He walked across the room and opened the closet door. There, next to her suitcase, lay her purse. He opened it and produced a passport. "Already taken care of."

She walked over to him, feeling as if she were participating in a spy movie. Things just kept happening around her, surprises around every corner. "But I've never had a passport," she told him, taking the black-bound item out of his hand.

"You do now."

She flipped it open. A black-and-white photo of her stared back.

"And a—"

"Visa?" he asked, producing it.

"How did you manage to get the passport and visa without my applying for them?"

He took them from her and put them back into her purse, zipping it shut. "We never divulge how." There was a trace of a smile at the corners of his mouth. "But sometimes the government can cut red tape as well as create it."

"Obviously," she muttered, still a little stunned. KGB agents were out looking for her. Why should the appearance of a little passport and visa throw her? Just because it normally took months to apply for a visa shouldn't be any reason to act surprised when it appeared magically within a few short hours.

"Well, if there's nothing else..." He began edging out of the room.

She could tell he was reluctant to leave. She could sense it and she felt pleased. Finally, he left and she was alone in the room—or so she hoped. The events of the day before had taught her not to trust anything completely, not even her own eyes.

Sheera walked over to the window and looked out, scanning the street below. She wondered if the agent who had tried to abduct her was still out there somewhere. The very thought brought a fresh chill to her. She undressed quickly and climbed in under the covers. She knew she wasn't likely to get much sleep, but at least she would try to rest.

THE NEXT THING she knew, there was a hand on her shoulder gently shaking her. Sheera bolted upright in bed, swinging wildly.

"Hey, wait a minute. I'm one of the good guys, remember?" Damien restrained her and calmly pushed her back. "Do you always wake up like that?"

"Only when I'm on spy missions," she grumbled. She couldn't remember falling asleep.

Her hair had fanned out on the pillow, looking like a copper cloud that had been caught in a whirlwind. He wondered if he would ever stop feeling attracted to her. "I didn't mean to startle you," he said, "but you didn't answer when I knocked."

In a rebound reaction to all the tensions she had endured the previous day, she had fallen sound asleep, she realized as she sat up, running her hand through her hair. "What time is it?" she asked.

"Time to get going."

"Don't you people ever give specific answers?" She looked up at him accusingly.

He was staring at her in fascination, and she became aware that the lacy design on the bodice of her nightgown revealed more than it hid. She drew the blanket up a little higher. Gone were last night's euphoric, romantic thoughts, as daylight brought her back to her senses. Now that she was sober, she should conduct herself with propriety, she told herself. "We're going to be in big trouble if you can't keep your mind on your work," she couldn't resist saying.

"I was just wondering what was going through Cari's mind when she packed that. It doesn't seem like a suitable nightgown for a woman to wear while visiting her maiden aunt."

"I don't have any other kind. How did you know my aunt never married?" He was about to answer when she held up her hand. "No, wait. Stupid question. You people know everything, don't you?"

"We try to," he answered, struggling to keep his eyes on her face. The sight of the lavender fabric clinging to her firm body had momentarily distracted him. Then his mind focused on the words she had just uttered. She didn't have any other kind. Did she wear them for someone?

What the hell do you care? All you're supposed to do is make sure you get in and out of Warsaw safely, not who she models her nightgowns for.

"I'd like to get up now," she said, waiting for him to leave. She reached for her robe and slipped her arms through the sleeves. "Can I do that without an audience?"

"Are you used to having one?" *Damn,* what was the matter with him?

His question put her off. More details with which to help catalog her? "Not in my bedroom," she answered too quickly.

Her reply brought a smile to his face. "Then you won't have one now."

He left her staring after him, wondering just what had transpired between them.

THE FLIGHT TO WARSAW was long and tedious. They had to change over in London, where they had to wait a good two hours for their connecting flight. Sheera had curbed her inclination to wander around the airport and stayed close to Damien. Everyone looked suspicious to her now: The woman sitting to one side, her head nodding as she dozed with a sleeping child in her lap, might be a spy. Over in the corner, the emaciated man in the beret and wearing an ill-fitting suit might be one, too. The world looked a good deal more frightening now than it had a couple of days ago. After all, a bag lady had turned out to be a stunning brunette. Sheera couldn't trust her senses anymore.

"Nervous?" Damien asked her, watching the way she scanned the airport crowd.

"No," she lied, lifting her chin defensively.

"Bad sign. Overconfidence makes for a sloppy agent," he whispered, teasing, into her ear.

Sheera bristled at the criticism. "I've never been accused of being sloppy," she answered.

He's not talking about hanging up your clothes, Sheera, she upbraided herself.

"Good. Keep it that way."

His breath curled around her ear, and she felt a rush of desire, forgetting her fears. These romantic lapses were melodramatic and silly, she cautioned herself sternly. What they were involved in was deadly serious. This was no time for her to have romantic thoughts.

She remembered how surprised her aunt had sounded when she had called her earlier that morning to tell her that they were coming. Damien had stood next to the phone booth as she made the call, but he might as well have been in the next room or down in the lobby. Sheera knew that, except for a word here and there, he understood little of what she was saying. She took a bit of satisfaction from that.

It had taken some time for her aunt to be brought to the phone. Having no phone of her own, Zofia Kaminska had to be rounded up by a neighbor's young son. The slightly distrustful voice that had finally met Sheera's ear had melted into a symphony of happy words once Sheera had convinced her aunt that it was really she.

"She'll be more than pleased to receive us," Sheera had said to Damien when she hung up the phone. Damien had only nodded his satisfaction.

SHEERA SHIFTED in her seat now, her body protesting over all the sitting she had been doing for the past eleven hours. Her kelly-green two-piece suit was acquiring permanent wrinkles, and the muscles in her lower back ached. Neither the music nor the movie whose dialogue poured out of her headset had done anything to alleviate the restless, achy feeling that had overtaken her.

"We'll be there soon," Damien assured her, glancing in her direction.

He had hardly moved a muscle since they boarded the plane. He looked cool and collected in his British-style gray suit. Wasn't he human? Probably not, she thought. They probably drained all the human components out of him in the first week.

"What did you say to your aunt?" he asked. The question came so quietly that she thought she hadn't heard correctly.

She turned. Looking at his face, she realized suddenly that the question must have been on his mind since her phone call. It bothered him not to have total control over everything, she thought with just a trace of smugness. *See how it feels,* she taunted him silently.

"Just what we'd agreed on," she said innocently. "I told her that we had gotten married and that we were coming to Poland to get her blessing. I also said that we'd be traveling through Europe on business."

"Wasn't she just the slightest bit surprised? You've never visited her before."

He knew that, too. She might have known he would. "No, not in person." She paused, letting him puzzle it out for a moment. "But we write all the time. And I have called her on occasion. Ever since my mother died, she's become more important to me, even though I've never met her face-to-face," she added, her voice growing more serious. "She's a crusty, talkative lady. She was five years older than my mother. Took her death awfully hard. She doesn't have any other relatives except for Judy and me. And Judy never got in touch."

She looked out the window. Dawn was creeping up, struggling to light the vast sky. She watched for a moment, fascinated. She had never paid much attention to sunrises and sunsets. There was always too much to do, and her mind was always elsewhere.

She had met three dawns in his company, she mused. How long would that continue? No philosophy before morning coffee, she warned herself. She couldn't think clearly without coffee.

Sheera stretched, then moved to rise. Damien caught her wrist just as her hand touched the headrest in front of her. Old habits were hard to break.

"Where are you going?" he asked.

"To the bathroom. Or do we do that together, too?" she asked.

He let her wrist go. "Sorry. Habit," he muttered.

She edged down the aisle, her eyes skimming over the bent and nodding heads on either side. Most people were trying to catch a few minutes of sleep before landing.

She saw someone start to rise, then quickly sink down as she drew closer. He averted his face. Curious, she focused her gaze on him.

Odd. Probably changed his mi— Sheera's heart began to hammer. It was the other KGB agent from the park!

The tranquillity she had just attained faded as quickly as did the last shadows of darkness.

Chapter Eleven

Sheera felt as if a blast of hot air had just hit her and for a moment she couldn't catch her breath. She turned quickly and hurried back to her seat.

Damien was surprised to see her back so soon. "Line too long?" he asked.

"He's here," she whispered.

She had turned pale. Damien sat up, alert. "Who's here?"

How many "he's" is he expecting, she thought impatiently. "The man from the park. The other KGB agent," she stressed, her voice low.

To her amazement, Damien appeared to be totally unconcerned. He relaxed again. "Yes, I know."

"You know?" She almost choked over the words. Throughout the trip there had been nothing in his manner to indicate the slightest bit of concern. He hadn't said a word to her about anyone following them.

"Well, what do we do about it?" She tried to keep her anxiety under control, feeling a bit disappointed with herself. She was overreacting. She should be calm, like him. Sheera glanced at his relaxed expression. She decided that she could never be that calm.

"At this altitude, nothing," he answered mildly.

"Very smart," she quipped. "But what about when we land?"

"Worry about it then."

"That's not exactly a very comforting plan."

He shrugged. "Best I can do at the moment."

"How long did you say you were in this business?" She hoped to hide her anxiety behind the barb.

She looked agitated, clutching the armrest so tightly that her knuckles were white. He placed his hand over hers. "There's nothing we can do until we get to the airport."

FLYING HAD NEVER BOTHERED SHEERA, but she hated takeoffs and landings. The pull of the plane as it increased or decreased altitude always gave her a queasy feeling in her stomach. She was feeling just that now, as they were landing.

And her stomach hadn't been doing too well to begin with. For the past hour she could think of little else but the agent who sat ten rows behind them. In her mind, the entire planeload of people had become an indistinguishable lump, and nothing existed but the agent. Before he reappeared she had begun to feel a little safer—out of sight, out of mind. But now she had to face reality again. She was in on this all the way. And the way was dangerous.

You asked for it.

Yes, she had, she thought. And it was time to see what kind of courage she possessed.

Sheera drew a deep breath. She could feel the plane slowing down. They had landed. "What happens in the airport?" she asked, taking a furtive glance over her shoulder. All she was could see was the tops of a few heads.

"We try to lose him."

"Very specific." There was no way to look through ten rows to see if he had shifted places. "Any ideas as to how?"

"Not yet."

"Comforting."

He still had his hand on top of hers and he gave her an additional squeeze, as if he were trying to reassure her. "It'll be all right."

"Of course it will," she answered. "We're the good guys. And the good guys always win, don't they?"

"That's what I always say." He winked.

Damien was out of his seat as soon as the seat-belt sign turned off. He took Sheera's hand. "Now" was all he said. The order was crisp, clear. It was enough.

Holding her traveling bag in one hand, she kept a firm grasp on Damien's hand with the other. They pushed their way through the slow-moving throng, muttering "excuse me" in exchange for complaints or curses thrown their way over their rude behavior.

Damien took no notice, moving constantly forward, his target the open door.

Sheera moved with him, ignoring the glares of the other passengers. Her body was buffeted by blows as she got in the way of paraphernalia that was being swung down from the overhead storage compartments. She kept ducking, mindful all the while not to lose her grip on Damien's hand.

The two look-alike blond stewardesses in blue flashed frozen smiles and said that they hoped Sheera and Damien would be back soon.

So do I, Sheera thought as they hurried into the airport itself.

"Now what?" Sheera asked.

"Customs."

"But he'll catch up," she protested, looking over her shoulder again. She couldn't see him, but she knew he was there. She stumbled as Damien pulled her along.

"Probably," he agreed. "But there's no way around it. The officials here don't look too kindly on people who try to circumvent having their luggage searched," he told her dryly.

Sheera nodded numbly as she fell into step, walking quickly in order to keep up.

They took their place in line and it gave her a moment to catch her breath. When her turn came, she watched silently as a large-pawed customs official sifted through her belongings, turning the neatly packed clothes into a rumpled mess. Satisfied that there was nothing there, he nodded curtly.

"Move on," he ordered, the heavily accented words spoken in English for her benefit. Then he leaned over to the uniformed man next to him and muttered something in Polish.

"What did he say?" Damien whispered as they walked away, his own suitcase already a victim of the other official's search.

Sheera kept her eyes straight ahead. "He told the other man he wished he'd had a reason to search me thoroughly as well." She heard Damien laugh softly.

"I know how he feels," he said under his breath.

He had muttered too low to hear. "What?"

"I said we'd better get out of here. Our friend seems content just to follow us."

"How do you know that?"

"If he wanted us, he'd be standing here, whispering in the custom inspector's ear."

Damn, he swore, how had the KGB known he was going to be on this plane? He tried to comfort himself with the thought that since the agent *was* following them, the defecting scientist hadn't fallen into the KGB's hands. If he had, the KGB wouldn't have bothered to follow him and Sheera. The agents would have gone directly to where the scientist had hidden the second half of the plans.

"He's watching us now," Damien told Sheera.

She looked around nervously. "Where is he?" She hadn't seen any sign of the hulking man since they had deplaned, but that didn't help matters any. Every face looked hostile to her. *Get hold of yourself, Sheera,* she ordered sharply, *before you become totally paranoid*.

"Over there, by the entrance." Damien kept his eyes in the opposite direction. Sheera began to look toward the entrance, but he steered her away. "Didn't you say you had to go to the ladies' room?" he reminded her.

What an odd thing to say at a time like this. She looked at him uncertainly. "Yes."

"Why don't you see if you can find where it is?" he suggested.

She was beginning to know him too well to take his suggestion at face value. "All right," she said slowly, waiting for more.

Damien said nothing more until Sheera located the rest room, which had a stick figure of a woman on its door. Opposite was the men's room.

"Why don't you see if you can get out the window," he said, his tone low and mild, as if he were suggesting something completely ordinary.

She stared at him. "What if it doesn't have a window?"

"We'll try something else." He made it sound as if he had a hatful of plans.

Sheera looked over his shoulder and saw that the KGB agent had been joined by another man. Both were now looking in their direction. *What are they waiting for,* she wondered. Whatever it was, she hoped they would go on waiting.

"If it does have a window, wait until the stalls are free, then climb out," he was saying. "I'll do the same." He nodded toward the men's room. "I'll meet you on the other side. If you're not there in ten minutes, I'll come back inside."

He made it sound so easy, she thought resentfully.

"And smile," he instructed, leaning close to her. "You look as if you'd seen a ghost."

"Not my own, I hope." She put on a bright smile, then turned and walked into the ladies' room.

There was only one occupant, a thin, round-shouldered woman whose blouse had been flung carelessly on the dilapidated wooden bench in the corner. The woman was washing her hair.

Sheera groaned inwardly and went into a stall. The first door had a broken latch. Sheera came out. She noticed that the woman, angling her head under the faucet, gave her a curious look.

"Doesn't work," Sheera muttered in Polish. She walked into the second stall. The door creaked as she shut it.

Sheera heard the woman shut off the water and then there were some shuffling noises. What was she doing? Was she really washing her hair, or had she been planted there?

Be reasonable. How would the woman have known that Sheera would go in there?

The sound of cursing penetrated the air. Sheera peered through the crack at the side of the door. She saw that the woman, her cropped black hair standing about her head like a wrinkled halo, was angrily winding up the cord of an inert hair dryer, which she then proceeded to throw into her suitcase. Probably operated on a different voltage, Sheera guessed, vaguely recalling tales of woe from friends who had gone to Europe only to find that the small electric appliances they had brought with them didn't work on a different voltage.

The woman, still muttering, zipped up her cloth suitcase and stormed out, her hair dripping.

Sheera was alone.

But for how long, she had no way of knowing. She looked at her watch. Four minutes had gone by. She wondered if Damien was already outside waiting for her, or if he had run into some obstacle himself. What if she got out and he wasn't there? Or she couldn't get out and he had?

"One thing at a time, Sheera," she told herself, trying to draw courage from the sound of her own voice.

There was a window in the bathroom, but it was covered with a thick coat of gray dust that must have taken years to form. The corners were streaked in yellow and brown, the results of countless rainstorms seeping through the rotted window sash. The windowsill was just at her chin level and, try as she might, she couldn't get a proper grip. She searched about frantically for something to stand on. The bench! But the bench appeared to be attached to the wall. Her spirits fell for a moment. *Well,* she thought, rallying, *everything else seems to have rotted away. Maybe the wood around the bolts had, too.*

She gave the bench a hearty tug and it came loose from the wall. Rusted bolts pointed accusingly at her from the wall like long, ugly fingers. She dragged the bench over to the window, hoping that the call to nature wouldn't overtake any of the other female passengers for another few minutes.

Climbing on the bench, Sheera could now easily reach the window. Opening it, however, was another story. The grit that covered the window also helped to seal it shut. She struggled with the sash, trying to lift it up. It refused to budge.

But something else did.

Too late, Sheera heard the door behind her. Someone was coming in. She whirled around, her cheeks hot with the flush of guilt. "I...felt faint and needed some air," she stammered in Polish.

The woman who heard these words was a nun dressed in the habit that had been so prevalent twenty years ago. Her flowing black robes almost touched the ground as she drew closer to Sheera. The nun, who had a large scar along her cheek, did not respond; only the click of her black shoes and the rhythmic sound of her rosary beads, swishing as she walked, could be heard.

For a moment, Sheera wasn't sure if the older women had understood her. She began to repeat herself when the nun smiled knowingly.

"You have much strength for a fainting woman," she said in English, smiling. Then her voice lowered. "Are they after you?"

"Who?" Sheera asked, pretending innocence.

The woman waved a wrinkled hand at her. And to Sheera's surprise, she lifted the hem of her flowing habit, displaying dark-stockinged legs, and agilely mounted the bench next to Sheera.

"Two pairs of hands are better than one," the nun said cheerfully.

When Sheera merely stood there, stunned, the nun turned to her. "God provides the strength, but we must provide the labor," she reminded her.

Roused, Sheera began to push at the window with all her strength. Together they managed to lift it. Sheera hoisted herself up onto the windowsill.

"Here, is this yours?" the nun asked, holding up Sheera's suitcase.

Sheera nodded. The older woman lifted the bag up and into Sheera's hands. "Go with God," she instructed, making the sign of the cross.

Sheera had no time to contemplate the nun's motives for helping her, for she suddenly felt someone grip her shoulder from behind. She whirled around, her suitcase ready to swing at whoever it was.

"It's me," Damien declared, jumping out of range. "You're going to have to do something about your nerves," he told her. He took the bag from her. She surrendered it gladly. "What kept you?"

"I think I did fairly well," she sniffed. "That was the first rest-room window I've ever climbed out of."

Damien took her hand and they hurriedly began walking down the street. But he was careful not to set too rapid a pace, since he didn't want to attract any undue attention.

"The window was stuck," Sheera explained. And then she added, "A nun helped me." She waited for the information to surprise Damien. It didn't.

"Whatever works," Damien said, crossing a narrow street.

Sheera gave up. "Where are we going?" she wanted to know.

"Away from the airport" was all he would say.

"But my aunt..." Sheera protested, suddenly remembering. "She said she'd be here." The appearance of the KGB agent had thrown everything else out of her mind for a while. "She'll be worried."

"She's waited this long to see you, she can wait a little longer," Damien told her. "Better than leading the KGB to her door."

"Good point." Sheera decided to stop arguing and just follow him.

Only he had stopped moving. "Do you know how to get to your aunt's house?" he asked suddenly.

Sheera nodded. "She told me on the phone, just in case she was late getting to the airport. But it's too far to walk from here."

"Let's find a taxi," he urged, scanning the area. "And when we go out again, maybe you should wear something a little less striking."

"Striking?" she echoed.

"You're turning people's heads, and right now I don't think that's too advisable," he commented. "We want to blend in."

"I wasn't the one who packed," she reminded him. "That was Cari's department." And then her tone sobered. "My aunt lives alone. There'll be no one to let us in," she pointed out. "And if I know my aunt, she'll be waiting at that airport until I show up."

He didn't appear to hear her. "Is that one?" Damien asked, pointing to what looked like an old-model Mercedes that had been preserved through the years with loving care.

"One what?" She was finding it difficult to keep up with his shifting train of thought.

"Taxi."

The car was some distance away, but it did appear to be a cab. "I think so."

Damien took her hand and they hurried across the street.

The man in the taxi was reading a newspaper, slumped back in his seat as if he had been sitting there, waiting, for a long time.

"Give him the address," Damien instructed.

Sheera asked the man if he was in service and if he could drive them to the address she specified.

A solicitous smile was on the man's unshaven face in an instant. The paper flew off to the side on the seat next to him and he leaped out of his car, opening the back door for them. He said something to Sheera.

"That's what I like," Damien said, "service."

"What he seems to like," Sheera said, "are American dollars."

"Oh?"

She grinned. "My aunt says they can smell Americans here. Americans are very good for the economy. That's why tourists are so welcome here. American dollars bring a high price on the black market."

"Your aunt deals in the black market?" Damien asked. Somehow he had pictured a short, squat little woman built something like a sturdy washtub. Sturdy washtubs didn't deal in the black market.

Sheera nodded. "Sure. Everyone here deals in it, even if they pretend not to. Goods are hard to come by, if not scarce altogether. If you have enough money, there's a lot you can get." She turned toward him, lowering her voice. "My aunt gets half her groceries through the black market."

"I thought you said she was poor. Where does she get the money?"

"She has a slight pension. I supply the rest."

Bascom would be surprised, Damien thought, to learn that those regular payments he had uncovered were being mailed to feed a fifty-nine-year-old woman. He grinned to himself.

"Did I say something funny?" Sheera asked, noticing his expression.

"Nothing that you'd understand," he said.

"There's a lot of that going around," Sheera muttered.

THE TAXI DRIVER let them off in an old, run-down neighborhood. A butcher shop was on the corner, and a line comprising predominantly women and old men extended halfway down the block. Each waited for his or her turn in the shop.

"That's my aunt's friend," Sheera said, nodding her head toward the butcher shop. "She wrote me all about him. He's the one with the telephone." They had alighted from the car in front of the ugly, squat gray tenement where Sheera's aunt lived. Parts of the exterior were crumbling. "Well, this is it. But I know she's down at the airport, waiting for us."

"When you called your aunt," Damien said, "you said that the man whose phone number you had called had sent someone to get her, didn't you?"

Sheera nodded. "His son."

"Maybe his son would like to earn a few American dollars?" Damien suggested.

Sheera grinned, relieved. She didn't like to think of her aunt sitting in the airport, worrying. The woman had been through enough in her lifetime.

So you're making her life easier by bringing her a spy. Nice going, Sheera.

"Worth a try," Sheera said to Damien.

They garnered a lot of strange looks—some curious, some wistful, others resentful—as they made their way to the butcher-shop entrance.

One woman thought they were trying to usurp her position in line and accosted them with a barrage of words until Sheera explained that they were visiting from America and only needed to speak with the proprietor.

"Mr. Lekawski?" Sheera said in Polish to the big, barrel-chested man behind the counter.

He looked harried and in no mood for any conversation that didn't have an order for meat in it.

"Yes?" he snapped at her.

"I'm Sheera O'Malley," Sheera continued in her mother's maiden tongue.

The fleshy jowls lifted in a smile, displaying an uneven row of stubby, yellowed teeth. "Sheera?" he echoed warmly. "Hanka!" he bellowed over his shoulder.

A thin, tall woman came scurrying out almost immediately, wiping her hands on a bloodied apron that hung down to her ankles. One shoulder strap lay at half-mast and she kept tugging it up almost constantly, fighting a battle she seemed destined to lose.

"What is it?" she asked her husband wearily.

"This is Sheera O'Malley!" the butcher proclaimed to everyone in the tiny store, gesturing at Sheera. The name brought an immediate smile of recognition not only from Hanka but also from several of the other women.

Damien suddenly found himself overwhelmed by the

chorus of strange words flying past his ears. He backed away for a moment, letting Sheera field the questions that came at her from all directions. He found himself engulfed by the growing throng.

Damn Stanislaus, Damien thought, wishing he could understand what was being said. Why did he have to pick this time to disappear?

Chapter Twelve

Zofia Kaminska was a surprise. Far from being built like an old-fashioned washtub, as Damien had envisioned, the woman looked like a much older version of Sheera. Her nearly wrinkleless face was filled with dignity, and she could still be regarded as a handsome woman. Her faded copper-colored hair had gray streaks running through it and was pulled back into a small knot at the nape of her neck. Several wisps had come loose as a result of her fast pace. She had come in hurrying behind the butcher's twenty-year-old son, muttering about being dragged all over Warsaw. But once she walked into the room and saw Sheera, the flow of words stopped abruptly.

Sheera and Damien were sitting at the end of a long wooden table. Most of the table was covered with different cuts of meat that Hanka was preparing. Several flies buzzed around, landing on one piece after another, only to be waved away by the butcher's wife. Hanka had kept up a steady stream of conversation with Sheera, leaving Damien to his own thoughts. He welcomed the other woman's entrance with a measure of relief.

"Sheera?" The name trembled in the air, floating in a sea of emotion.

Sheera turned to see the woman standing uncertainly in the doorway. Tears were shimmering in her eyes. Sheera walked over to her quickly. *"Tak, Ciociu, to ja,"* she said, confirming her identity for her aunt.

Aunt Zosia silently enfolded Sheera in her arms. She held on to her as if Sheera were a long-lost child.

Damien stood by his chair, quietly allowing them their moment. He was the only quiet one in the room. Everyone else was talking at the pair at once. He shoved his hands deep in his pockets, frustrated. He hated not knowing what was going on. He might have committed a map of the city to memory and know the local customs inside out, but his grasp of the language was horribly lacking. All he had to rely on was Sheera's word for what was happening until Stanislaus showed up. *If* Stanislaus showed up. What if Sheera became confused? It made him uneasy.

"And this," the woman continued in Polish, looking toward Damien, "is your husband?"

Sheera stepped back, linking her fingers through his. She drew him forward with just the right touch of enthusiasm. He wondered where she had learned to act so well.

"Yes, Aunt, this is my husband, Damien," Sheera answered, the Slavic words sounding soft and romantic on her lips. For effect, she rested her head against his shoulder.

"Don't overdo it," Damien said between rigid lips.

He smiled at Sheera's aunt, then took her hand and kissed it. He was acquainted with enough European women to know that the custom was still enjoyed, still looked upon favorably. He noted that the woman looked at him for a long moment and saw suspicion in her eyes.

"She doesn't appear to like me," Damien said to Sheera, still keeping his smile intact. "Does she dislike capitalists?"

It was a flippant remark he hadn't expected Sheera to answer. He certainly hadn't expected her aunt to answer—in English.

"On the contrary, I like capitalists very much." The words were heavily accented. "I am trying to decide whether I like you very much."

"You speak English?" Damien asked, surprised. He cast a questioning look toward Sheera.

"It would appear so," Aunt Zosia answered.

"It never occurred to me that you didn't know," Sheera explained to Damien, palms extended upward in helpless apology.

Aunt Zosia moved about him in a semicircle, surveying him as if he were a piece of goods. Behind her, Hanka, the butcher's wife, was offering a running commentary of her own thoughts about the American.

Hanka kept her tone respectful, Sheera noticed, but the warmly appraising, hungry look in her eyes said far more than her lips did. She wondered if Hanka's restraint arose from her respect for Aunt Zosia or from her fear of being overheard by the burly man in the front of the store.

Damien bore it all patiently, Sheera thought. But then, what choice did he have?

"Do they speak English, too?" Damien asked Aunt Zosia as she came around full circle. He was nodding at Hanka and her son. The latter was still fingering in his pocket the American dollars that Damien had given him for fetching Sheera's aunt. He was grinning from ear to ear.

"No, they do not have a reason to," Aunt Zosia answered. "They have no one in America." She turned and smiled at Sheera. "I do."

Damien got the distinct impression that the connection put the woman in a favored position in the community.

Aunt Zosia took both of Sheera's hands in hers. "How much you look like your mother," she said, tears springing up again. "She was a beauty."

"Ah, would you mind if we went to your apartment now, Madame Kaminska?" Damien prodded. Hanka had moved in closer and was now running a very heavy hand over his jacket.

Sheera suppressed a grin, wondering if the woman's prime interest was the material or what lay beneath it. Damien purposely avoided Sheera's wide grin, looking, instead, toward Aunt Zosia.

"Of course. Of course." The slender woman turned toward the door and led them out. "What happened?" she asked Sheera suddenly. "Why were you not at the airport? I waited, just as you said."

"We were at the airport," Damien cut in smoothly, since Sheera looked lost for words. "But somehow we seemed to have missed each other. Sheera thought perhaps you were ill and couldn't come to meet the plane."

"Ill?" Aunt Zosia echoed in wonder. "I have not been ill a day in my life. You know that."

"Yes, I do, Aunt," Sheera said, taking the woman's hand in hers. "But stranger things can happen." She gave Damien a triumphant smile, showing him that she could pick up his cues.

Getting past the crowd in the front of the store took a long time. They were engulfed by a new sea of hands extended in greeting. Everyone, it seemed, knew her aunt, Sheera thought. And everyone wanted to meet her relatives from America.

Sheera kept a smile on her face, nodding and returning greetings, wondering all the while if these simple people were everything they appeared to be. She was more anxious than Damien to get to her aunt's apartment.

"They like to make a fuss," Aunt Zosia said high-handedly as she moved down the street, waving and nodding like reigning royalty to the passersby. "I hope you do not mind. I have told them all about you for so long that they feel they know you."

The sidewalk was badly cracked in several places, as were the buildings that were around them. Aunt Zosia patted the gaping hole forming by the door of her building. "Nothing like wood, I have always said." She shook her head.

The apartment was claustrophobic, Sheera thought, looking around as her aunt led them inside. There was barely enough room to turn around in the tiny kitchen-and-living-room area. What room there was was taken up by a few possessions, the cherished accumulations of a lifetime. The walls were all covered with pictures, both faded and new. The frames were dustless, as if lovingly cared for each day.

One faded brown-and-white framed photo caught Sheera's eye.

"Is this my mother?" Sheera asked, walking over to it. A bright-faced girl in long braids stood next to a slender young woman.

A short nod answered her question. "Yes, that was her. A beautiful child. A beautiful woman." The words were accompanied by a huge sigh.

Sheera thought her aunt was going to cry again, but then the clear blue eyes looked at her crisply. "Come, I will show you where to put your things."

The only other room in the house was the bedroom. It appeared even smaller than the other room. A bed with a thick floral printed quilt and a bureau took up almost all the available space.

"You will sleep here," Aunt Zosia announced.

Sheera stole a glance at Damien. She could see that the sleeping arrangements suited him fine. This time there was no sofa to send him to. Well, she'd handle that somehow when the time came.

Sneaking another glance at Damien, she knew how he would like to handle the situation.

"Now, you must be hungry."

Sheera realized that her aunt hadn't meant it as a question. It was a statement. She was about to demur when she thought better of it. The woman had no one to fuss over and it would do her good to do so, at least for a little while. It might make up, in part, Sheera thought, a flash of guilt nipping at her, for the deception that she was putting her aunt through. Sheera didn't like lying to her, but there was no choice in the matter.

"I have been cooking and baking since you called," Aunt Zosia said cheerfully, then went back into the kitchen.

"Nice bed," Damien murmured as Sheera edged past him to get to the door.

"Nice cover," she countered. "You get that. On the floor."

"We'll see." He grinned at her.

"No, we won't," she said firmly.

Aunt Zosia turned the gas jet on. A huge pot emitted a protest. "Everything should be ready very soon," she promised.

She gestured toward the kitchen table, the center of life within the house, indicating that they should take their seats.

Sheera complied, trying to keep her mind off the bed in the other room and the possible problem it presented. Damien sat down next to her, smiling quietly to himself. He wasn't fooling her, she thought. He was enjoying her predicament. This was something she hadn't even thought of when she had fabricated their cover story so quickly back at the hotel. Then she had been desperate not to be left behind. Now she was growing desperate for another reason.

"So, tell me, how did you meet and why did you marry so soon?" The clear blue eyes probed Sheera's face, waiting for an answer.

Sheera took a breath, then recited the answer that they had rehearsed back in New York. Quick to respond to Sheera's bright idea, Damien had created an entire history of their whirlwind courtship and marriage. Sheera rattled it all off with the proper intonation. She was proud of herself for remembering the details. She watched her aunt's face to see if there were any traces of disbelief.

But the woman seemed to take it all in, nodding her head in empathy several times.

"Ah, that reminds me of myself as a young girl. Yes, believe it or not, I, too, was young once." She winked. Damien was willing to bet that she had really been something then. A real hell-raiser. "Why, I remember once..." She launched into a story.

THREE HOURS LATER, the meal had been served and eaten, and Aunt Zosia was still talking. Sheera shifted in her seat, wanting to cut her aunt short but not knowing just how to do it without being rude. Damien, for his part, hadn't said very much. But Sheera could tell that he was anxious to get going.

Her own sense of urgency derived from the knowledge that there was still a KGB agent out there somewhere dogging their trail. They had temporarily lost him that morning, but she did not fool herself. Those people had tenacity. She had no doubt that the man would turn up again, probably with reinforcements.

Had she left her aunt open to trouble, she wondered suddenly, feeling uneasy. She had to talk to Damien about that.

Aunt Zosia's seemingly endless flow of words finally stopped. The pile of potatoes she had been peeling tottered as she put the last one on top. "What is wrong?" she asked.

"Nothing," Sheera lied. "I was just wondering if perhaps we could get a little sightseeing in today. I'm afraid we're not going to be here that long and I wanted to see some of the places Mother always talked about."

Aunt Zosia looked toward the window, then waved a hand. "It is going to rain any moment. Sightseeing in the rain is not a very good thing. Tomorrow. You can go sightseeing tomorrow. Today, we talk."

Today, Damien thought, *she* talked. He wondered if Zofia Kaminska was just a harmless woman, hungry for company, or if she was more than she seemed.

THE STORM that Aunt Zosia had predicted brewed darkly in the sky as angry clouds gathered, then finally erupted in rain. It rained hard, sending a chill into the spring air.

"I am sorry," Aunt Zosia apologized, "but how do you say...?" She looked at Sheera.

Sheera waited to hear the Polish word she was being asked to translate but her aunt found the English equivalent herself.

"The landlord," Aunt Zosia said, spitting out the name. "He shuts off the heat when April comes. Cold April or warm April, makes no difference to him. He tries to make a little off the poor people."

Damien raised a brow toward Sheera. Her aunt's sentiments did not sound very much like the ones that should be coming from a good communist.

He said as much to Sheera when Aunt Zosia went to the closet to fetch a sweater.

"That's because she isn't," Sheera answered, carrying the potatoes to the sink. "She's resented their takeover ever since World War Two. She was part of the Resistance during the war. One of the youngest fighters they had," Sheera added with a touch of pride.

"Then why doesn't she leave?" It didn't make any sense to him. "You could sponsor her." It seemed too unusual a situation to him. Given the option himself, he would have seized it.

"At my age, how could I start over again?" Aunt Zosia asked, having heard him. "Do not be deceived. Just because I am not as young as you does not mean that my hearing has gone to sleep. I hear—and see— plenty." She gave him a broad wink. Damien felt himself being charmed. "But there are other things to consider besides the freedom to come and go as I please.

They leave older people alone here. And I have my friends. I have lived in this house for over thirty years. There is comfort in that."

She turned her attention to Damien. "And what is it you said you do?" she asked.

He hadn't, but he told her now. "I'm a salesman."

"What kind of a salesman?" Aunt Zosia pressed, stopping Sheera from pouring off the water. "No, they will turn brown if you do that," she chided.

He got the distinct impression that despite the fact that she was talking to Sheera, the woman was scrutinizing him very carefully. Again, he wondered if she was as harmless as she appeared. "I'm a computer salesman."

Aunt Zosia shook her head, not liking his answer. "You had better not say that around here. It may reach the ears of one of our government officials. Their minds are so narrow, it might give them cause to be suspicious."

"I thought you said it was comfortable here," Damien remarked.

"The older people, they are comfortable," Aunt Zosia clarified, setting the potatoes aside and turning her attention to something else. "The young ones, they have not made up their minds where they want to be. They yearn for blue jeans from America but feel they should give their loyalty to the party. After all, it is all they were taught from the cradle on. Now that some start to think by themselves, it is not so clear to them anymore. But you cannot take any chances."

No, they couldn't, Sheera thought. Certainly not even to allow her aunt to learn why they were really there. As far as the woman was to know, they were just stopping by for a few days on their way through Poland.

"Well, it is time for me to go to sleep," Aunt Zosia said, stretching. She trudged to a narrow linen closet and pulled out a worn blanket. Pushing the doors closed with her back, she proceeded to the sofa to make up a bed. "I will sleep here. You will sleep there." She pointed to her room.

"But—" Sheera began.

"Do not argue with me," Aunt Zosia said firmly. "Young married people belong together. Sleeping apart is what leads to problems. Trust me." She patted her chest. "I know these things. Many a marriage I have seen fall by the wayside because of this." She fairly pushed Sheera into the bedroom. "Go, sleep. Or whatever."

"I like your aunt," Damien said once the door was closed.

Sheera looked at the grin on his face. "You would." She took a deep breath. "All right, what do we do about the sleeping arrangements?" she asked.

"Enjoy them." He came up behind her and put his hands on her shoulders. She could feel his breath on her neck as he lowered his head.

"That's not quite what I had in mind," she said, the words faltering on her tongue.

"No?" A kiss feathered down along her neck. "Funny, that's what I've had in my mind for quite some time now."

She twisted around, trying to get away from the damaging effect of his lips on her neck. "You're awfully blasé for a man in a foreign country who doesn't know what's going on."

His eyes were disarming her quickly. "I know exactly what's going on."

"Oh?" She swallowed. Her throat felt very dry. It was almost the only part of her that did. Her palms were damp. Nerves, she told herself.

"Right now," he said softly, kissing the other side of her throat, "we're getting ready for bed."

"We're getting ready for an argument," she parried, twisting away from him.

But his arms recaptured her with little effort. She had to admit that she was feeling less and less inclined to struggle.

"Your aunt would be very upset to find out that we're having our first marital spat." He drew her closer to him. She could feel the heat of his body transmitting itself to hers. It definitely took the edge off her resistance.

"You're really enjoying this, aren't you?" she tried to make it sound like an accusation but wasn't very successful.

"Not nearly as much as I'd like to be."

The words were soft, sultry, and Sheera found herself melting into them. The attraction that she had felt for him all along began to blossom, overpowering her common sense. Getting involved with this man had no future in it. And Sheera knew that once she did get involved, she couldn't just go merrily on her way. She wasn't the type. Cool, collected, calm in a boardroom crisis, Sheera was still tremendously vulnerable when it came to her emotions. She didn't believe in casual affairs. Making love meant loving. It wasn't merely an exercise in momentary satisfaction.

There was nothing momentary about the way she was feeling right now. Her need for him had been building within her like so much kindling being stored up. And now, now he was lighting a match to set it all aflame.

Damien didn't know exactly what had released the restraining shackles he had imposed on himself. Perhaps it was finding himself alone with her in such a small space. The smell of her perfume filled his senses and almost made it impossible to think of anything else but her. Perhaps it was because they were both so vulnerable now, living a temporary lie in a foreign country. Whatever it was, Damien found he could no longer resist her, could no longer fight his own desire. He needed her the way he needed the very air to breathe.

Sheera tried to back away. There was little room to move and she fell against the bed.

"I had no intention of proceeding that quickly," he said with a twinkle in his eye, "but if you insist..." He moved to lie down next to her.

Maybe he was only teasing, but she was taking no chances. Sheera scrambled up. "I—I don't insist," she stammered. "I mean I do..."

His grin was infuriating. "You're a complicated woman, Sheera O'Malley."

"The only complication in my life came when you ran into me," she told him, pulling her skirt down to cover the thighs that had been exposed to his appraising gaze.

"I believe you were the one who ran into me," he reminded her.

"Believe what you want. That's irrelevant."

"Is it?"

"It is right now." She put her feet down on the other side of the bed. There was exactly one foot between her and the window. He came around and closed off her exit.

Trapped, she thought.

Code Name: Love 167

Somehow, the word did not hold as much terror for her as it normally did. As a matter of fact, there was no terror at all. This was crazy. She tried desperately to draw fuel from her claustrophobic feelings. It had vanished. In its place was longing.

Damn it, her own body was turning on her, yearning for his.

He brushed her hair away from her neck, his fingertips caressing her face. "Sheera, why did you follow me?"

"Strange time to be playing secret agent," she whispered.

He kissed her forehead gently. Sheera felt her knees giving way. *You're a grown woman,* she insisted, trying to strengthen herself against this onslaught.

Yes, a voice whispered back, *a grown woman with a woman's longings.*

"No, this answer is for me, not for any form or information bank." The words tickled her skin as he continued kissing her.

"I told you, I saw that man take your briefcase." Coherent thoughts were getting harder and harder to form.

"You were following me before that."

"I—" He had worked his way to her throat again. Her pulse hammered there, mimicking the rhythm of her rapid heartbeat. "I wanted to take a walk. It was a nice day and—"

"Is it so hard to admit to your feelings, Sheera?" he asked, his lips barely touching the planes of her throat.

Sheera felt her stomach quivering. It felt just like when she took off in an airplane.

"And...what...makes...you...think...I have...any feelings...for...you?"

"Your eyes." He kissed each lid separately.

She was losing ground rapidly, she thought. His mouth covered hers before she had a chance to say anything to deny his assumption or defend herself. He was too sure of himself, damn him, too good at what he was doing to her right now.

How many other women had he seduced this way? It seemed a better way to while away the time than watching old movies on television. Especially since there was no television set there.

Thunder echoed through the room. The beat of her heart matched it, measure for measure. She felt his hands travel up the sides of her body, slipping from her waist and going to either side of her breasts. Her breath caught in her throat, then came in rapid spurts.

"You're taking advantage of the situation," she murmured helplessly against his mouth.

"You bet I am," he answered, the words vibrating from his lips onto her skin as he kissed the hollow of her throat. "It's what I was trained to do."

"Seduce women?"

"Make the most of my opportunities," he answered.

He moved his hands along her rib cage, stroking rhythmically, going higher and higher at each pass, until Sheera didn't think she could bear the wait any longer. But any movement on her part would let him know that she was now open to his invitation.

As if he had any doubts, she mocked herself. He was too experienced not to know that she was his for the taking.

Damn it, you're your own woman, Sheera, she argued with herself, trying to draw away. No, she had lied. She wasn't her own woman. She was his. And sinking fast.

"I really...wish you wouldn't...do this...."

To her surprise, he stopped kissing her. The crystal-blue eyes looked deeply into hers, as if trying to discern the truth. "Really, Sheera?" he whispered.

It gave her a moment's respite, a moment her body didn't welcome even if her mind did. "Would you stop?"

There was a beat and she thought he was struggling with himself, as if there was an internal war going on. "Yes," he finally answered.

Then say yes, her mind urged. *Tell him to stop before it's too late.*

"No," she said softly, "I lied."

"I hope it's the only lie you ever tell me," he said, lowering his mouth over hers again.

The way he said it, he made it sound as if he thought they were going to be together for a long time. *Idiot, what do you expect him to say, "I'll give you your walking papers once I've satisfied myself"?* Under the circumstances, he couldn't say anything else.

Logic refused to make her stop, yet didn't let go enough for her to fully abandon herself to what was happening to her.

He was an accomplished lover. Sheera had no real yardstick to go by. The few instances she had been with a man, however, could not even begin to compare to what she experienced with Damien. She would never have guessed that beneath his devil-may-care exterior there existed a man so gentle, so patient, so loving. Giving her pleasure seemed to be the uppermost thing in his mind. She could tell that he was restraining himself. She felt the bridled passion of his kiss, felt the fire that was being kept under control.

It served to fuel her own fire, her own desire.

The storm outside their window paled in comparison.

Chapter Thirteen

Morning brought with it a sobriety that had been missing the night before. Sheera stirred, then slowly opened her eyes, wondering what on earth she had allowed herself to do last night.

Damien was propped up on his elbow, looking down at her. A strand of her hair was curled about his fingers. He brought it to his lips.

"Good morning," he said softly. The strand of coppery hair dropped from his finger as he lowered his head and kissed the rounded corner of her shoulder. Sheera worked hard to restrain the shiver that seized her. "You were smiling in your sleep just now. Dreaming of me?"

"I—I don't remember," she lied. Oh God, what had she gone and done?

"Let me help prod your memory," he offered gently, his lips sensuously close to hers.

And then he was kissing her again.

Her reaction was immediate, even before she could clearly focus her mind. She wrapped her arms around his neck and pulled him closer, returning his kiss. Her body grew warm and rosy once again.

This was crazy and she knew it. There was no future in loving a spy. The ludicrousness of the whole thing hit her. The past few days of her life, if put on paper, would read like a grade-B spy thriller. Yet she was really living all this. She was fully awake now.

He had done this to her, she thought accusingly. A flood of thoughts washed through her mind. What was this? Thursday? No, Friday. It was hard to believe that three—no, four—days ago, she had been standing in the Roosevelt Avenue station, feeling bored. And now here she was in Poland, in bed with a spy.

My God, she had only known him four days and look at her.

Actually, she realized, she didn't know him at all. All she knew was what he did to her every time she was near him.

But she didn't care.

The phrase "Eat, drink and be merry" floated through her mind. Her lips parted from his for a moment, a twinkle playing in her eyes. "Let's be merry."

He stared at her for a moment, confused, but pleased with her response.

He asked no questions.

The word "ecstasy" gained a new depth.

"WE'D BETTER GET GOING," he whispered into her hair. She lay nestled in the protective circle of his arms, her head resting against his chest. She gently ran her fingertips along the soft, light hairs that feathered along his chest, tracing the rigid muscles beneath them.

"Yes," she said, sighing, "I guess we'd better."

Who would have ever guessed that she would have found love in a bed halfway around the world, she mused. Or was this all the way around the world? Right now, she didn't know. She couldn't remember her geography. She seemed unable to think about a lot of things, things she knew had to be faced soon. But not now. Definitely not now.

WHEN THEY CAME OUT of their room, Aunt Zosia flashed them a knowing smile. "I was starting to think that perhaps you would spend the day in bed." She walked over to Sheera and touched her cheek tenderly. "Did you sleep well?"

"Yes, thank you, Aunt." She stole a glance at Damien, who was moving toward the kitchen table.

"Come, I make you breakfast," Aunt Zosia said, indicating that Sheera should join Damien.

"Is there anything I can—" Sheera began, only to be shooed away.

"No, you are a guest in my house. A welcome, beloved guest. You sit, I work," Aunt Zosia insisted. She bobbed her head philosophically. "That is all I have done for all my life. That is what I do now." She stopped talking for a moment, looking from one face to the other. "You know, Damien, when I first saw you, I was not so sure. Now I am."

Sheera's pulse quickened. What did her aunt mean? Did she somehow suspect?

All Damien said was a casual "Oh?"

He was far cooler than she was, she thought, wishing she could tap some of his blasé attitude. Was he that way about everything, she wondered. Would he be that way about them when the time came?

"Yes, I was not so sure," Aunt Zosia repeated, moving on to the dark black box that passed for a stove, "that you were the right one for my little Sheera. But now, looking at her eyes, I know you are."

Sheera lowered her head and stared at the tabletop. She traced the heavy wooden grain with her forefinger.

She wished her aunt would keep her speculations to herself. It was bad enough that she had given herself to him so easily without her aunt saying that it was written all over her face. Sheera half expected to hear Damien chuckle. To her relief, he didn't.

"Same look I see in yours." Aunt Zosia waved a wooden spoon at Damien.

Now the chuckle came. Or was that a cough? Sheera tried to look at Damien's face, but he had averted it.

Breakfast consisted of a hearty serving of oatmeal, which Sheera could readily have done without. She promised herself to send her aunt more money if she got out of this. No one should have to face the morning on oatmeal, she thought, threading her spoon through the thick mass in her bowl.

"Well, I must go and do my shopping," the woman informed them, removing her apron. "I am afraid I shall be gone for quite some time. The lines..." She let her voice trail off as she shook her head. "Sometimes, I feel that I have been waiting on lines all of my life." She put on a large, flapping tweed coat. A bright blue scarf adorned her head. "When I come back, we talk some more, eh?"

She patted Sheera's cheek, then glanced at the half-finished bowl of oatmeal. "Eat. You are too thin."

"But you're thin," Sheera pointed out.

"I have no one to hold on to my body. You do." She winked.

With that, she left.

Sheera waited for half a beat, then was on her feet, the bowl in her hand. She poured the oatmeal down the sink, then began to dispose of the subsequent mess by running water over it. The lumps refused to dissolve. She mashed them down with her spoon.

"I thought it was good," Damien said, coming up behind her with his own bowl, empty.

Sheera shivered. "One more bite and I would have thr— Well, never mind what I would have done. I've got to send her more money so she can have a decent breakfast. Bacon and eggs."

"Eggs are high in cholesterol."

"They're also high in taste." She turned off the water and put away the bowl. "Oatmeal tastes like cooked soft, wet cement."

"Eat a lot of cement?"

"You're making fun of me," she accused.

"Yes." He drew her into his arms and gave her a quick kiss. "It's a dividend I allow myself every so often. Keeps the tension from getting to me." He made a move to kiss her again, then thought better of it. Once he started that, they weren't going to leave the apartment. "Better get your coat before your aunt comes back. We've got to get going."

"She won't be back for a long time," Sheera told him, walking into the bedroom for her things. She brought out her light tan coat and pushed her arm through one dolman sleeve. "She was right when she said she'd be gone half the day." Damien helped her into the other sleeve. "Thank you." She nodded. "That's how they do their shopping here, standing on one line after another. There are no such things as express lines here. And each item seems to be in a different store. Supermarkets would be heaven for them."

He was smiling indulgently at her and she realized how naive she was being, explaining all this to him. He knew better than she did the machinations of society in this country, or any country, for that matter, she'd wager.

Sheera fell silent, wondering what he thought of her. Not just for her naiveté, but in general. Did last night mean to him what it did to her? He had said beautiful, lovely things to her, but they had been said in the heat of the moment. Had they melted away now, like chocolate that had been left out in the sun too long?

"Wait, I want to leave a note," Sheera said, searching in her purse for a piece of paper.

"Tell her we've gone sightseeing."

Sheera wrote the words down, then joined Damien at the door. "Just what sights are we going to see?" she asked as they walked out onto the stoop.

The day was grayer than the day before. A general murkiness had settled over everything. Sheera looked up at the sky. The sun was completely hidden by dull, thick clouds.

"Actually," Damien answered, taking hold of her elbow as they walked down the concrete stairs, "the sight I'd most like to see is right next to me."

She smiled, pleased with his remark, even though, she thought, he probably meant nothing by it.

"But the one you're to see...?" She let her voice trail off expectantly.

"Is somewhere out there." He pointed vaguely to the surrounding area.

She knew that he had a far more specific handle on it than that. He was still being elusive. "We just made love until three in the morning," she began.

He glanced at her and raised a quizzical brow. "You timed it?"

He was trying to sidetrack her. She sighed impatiently. "I just happened to glance at my wristwatch. What I am trying to say is that we've been...intimate—"

"Very."

She ignored the warm, teasing smile on his lips. They walked past a cluster of uniformed elementary-school girls. Sheera lowered her voice. "We've been intimate," she repeated for emphasis, "and you still don't trust me."

The look on his face sobered just a little. "It's not a matter of trusting you. The less you know, the less dangerous you are to yourself."

"Or you," she interjected.

"That, too."

"I didn't think you were that altruistic," she said, pleased that she had gotten him to admit something.

"Altruism has its place," he pointed out. "So does survival. I want to live to have grandchildren."

Sheera's breathing quickened for a moment as she looked at him, stunned. "I didn't realize that you ever planned to get married."

The smile he gave her was light, easy. "I didn't say that."

"I didn't think so," she said, looking forward again. "I should have known better," she muttered to herself.

She might have known. He was the type to go scattering his seed all through the world. A slight trace of bitterness haunted her. She crossed her arms in front of her and pulled them tightly against her chest. It suddenly seemed chillier.

"Why?" He sounded only mildly interested in her speculations.

"You're not the marrying kind."

She expected him to agree. Instead, he said, "Oh? Have me all figured out, do you?"

She looked at him, hostility flaring within her veins. What else could she logically expect from a man like this? Charm, excitement and sensuality did not mix with loyalty and dependability. But did loyalty and dependability always have to mean boring, she thought glumly. "Pretty much so, yes."

He surprised her by saying softly. "I don't fit into pigeon holes, Sheera. I might just surprise you."

She wondered what he meant by that.

SHE HAD NEVER DONE so much sightseeing in her life. Damien, to her surprise, knew exactly where he was going without glancing down at the guidebook that Murphy had given her before they left and that she now clutched in her hand. They went through the Old Town first. A total shambles after the war, it had been painstakingly reconstructed according to old prints and paintings, predominantly those of Bernardo Bellotto, called Canaletto. Warm pastel colors were everywhere, giving the city a distinctive Old World flavor. The flavor was enhanced by a replica of the city's old cobblestoned marketplace, Rynek Miasta, with its colorful house fronts, uneven roofs and wrought-iron grillwork. Churches, palaces and burghers' houses throughout the area created a world that seemed untouched by time. Motorized traffic was barred from the area, completing the effect.

Sheera watched Damien carefully. But he merely acted like a tourist out to see as much as he could. They covered an incredible amount of ground.

Three hours later, Sheera was ready to call a halt to the sightseeing. Her feet hurt and, for all she knew, they were no closer to their destination than when they had started out. Certainly, Damien gave no indication that they were. She had no idea that Damien was trying to make sure that, if they were being followed, this exhausting traipse through the city would succeed in losing their shadow. The only hint she had gotten of the purpose of their visit was when he took her by the Palace of Culture and Science, a building, she knew, shunned by many Warsaw citizens. The wedding-cake skyscraper was a personal gift to the city from Stalin.

"He worked there," Damien told her when they stopped at a street named Marszalkowska. Given the location, she didn't have to ask who "he" was. Damien was talking about the scientist.

The rest of the day was devoted to museums. But they never stayed in one long enough to get more than a sampling of its flavor. Damien made a point of leaving each by any unattended side exit he found.

"What are we doing in the Frederick Chopin Museum?" she whispered into his ear, standing on her toes.

"Looking."

Sheera sighed. He'd tell her when he was ready. All she could do was wait. And see the sights.

"I'm beginning to feel like a rat in a maze," she complained, as they left one of the summer palaces located in Lazienki Park. "Can't we stop to have something to eat?" she asked.

"Should have finished your oatmeal," he teased.

"The oatmeal would have finished me," she informed him. Being so hungry made her feel waspish and her stomach was growling. That, added to the fact that she was annoyed with his lack of trust, didn't put her in the best humor. "So, can we stop to eat?" she asked again.

"Soon," he told her.

"How soon?" she pressed.

"There's a nice little café just across the river."

"The Vistula?" she asked incredulously.

"Is there another?" he asked mildly.

She didn't need wry humor at the moment, she thought unkindly. "C'mon," she said, resigning herself as she took his arm, "let's see if we can find a bus to take us over the bridge."

The small café was located at the corner. Most of its tables were outside and circled the end of the block, a street called Targowa. On one side, the tables faced an oppressive-looking school. On the other side, they faced a public rest room. Not the most appetizing setting, Sheera thought, instinctively walking toward the side that faced the school.

"Over here," he instructed softly, taking a seat at a table on the other end.

"Not much for atmosphere, are you?" she commented as she sat down. Her body telegraphed its thanks as she sank against the chair's wrought-iron back.

"Beauty is in the eye of the beholder."

She did not respond, knowing that it would only lead to more double-talk.

A tired-looking middle-aged man came up to them, a servile look stamped on his face. He stood waiting, his head and hands moving in sudden small jerks.

Damien ordered coffee, smugly content to have remembered the word in Polish.

Sheera also ordered coffee and asked for a tart besides.

The man shook his head emphatically and told her they had no tarts.

Sheera sighed and tried again. He finally wrote down her third choice.

"So much for the bounties of the system," she commented dryly as the man shuffled off. "He said they're out of practically everything. There's another food shortage and all the small cafés have been hit hard. Only the larger-name restaurants have gotten away unscathed." She gave him the information, hoping that he would offer to take her to one.

She could see that he wasn't paying attention to her. She was getting used to that, she thought irritably. He looked particularly intent, she thought. Something was up. She could sense it.

She decided right then and there that they were not meant for each other. Last night had been just a wonderful interlude in her life and a recreational break in his. Work would always be uppermost in his life. It had to be. He'd pay with his life for any lapses.

"Is anyone following us?" she asked in a low voice. If anyone was, that would account for the zigzag pattern they had taken today and for the way he was now studiously staring out ahead of him.

"What makes you ask that?"

"Oh, I don't know," she said flippantly. "It might have something to do with being chased in Central Park, having someone almost kidnap me at gunpoint in the heart of Manhattan, having the same strange man follow us on board a plane heading for Warsaw—shall I go on?" she asked sarcastically.

"No, I think you made your point." He still didn't look at her.

She felt like shaking him by the shoulders. "Look," she said, sliding to the edge of her seat, "I'm risking my life as much as you're risking yours," she pointed out. "If something goes wrong, I'm not going to be given a twenty-question quiz to determine how much I know or don't know. They thought I was with you even when I wasn't. They're certainly not going to give me the benefit of the doubt now. Now I want to know what we're doing here."

He finally turned to look at her. His expression told her that he was surprised by her question. Sheera struggled to hold on to her temper. "You said you wanted to stop and eat, remember?"

She held her tongue while a pair of lovers strolled by, smiling as if they were oblivious to everything else but themselves. Damien was relieved to see that Sheera was taking no chances.

"There were plenty of restaurants on the other side of the river," she pointed out once the couple was out of earshot. "Why didn't we stop at any one of them? Why here? And don't tell me it's the atmosphere," she warned.

"All right, I won't."

Finally, she thought.

"We're waiting for someone."

"Who?" she pressed.

"An interpreter."

Sheera bristled. "But I'm your—you don't trust me, do you?" she accused.

"I never said that," he said quietly.

"You don't have to," she said, setting her jaw hard. His distrust hurt all the more after the night they had spent together, after the fantasies she had let herself entertain. She stared straight ahead, blocking out everything around her.

You asked for it. All of it. You asked to be included, she reminded herself. *You asked to come trudging along on all this.* Well, that had been partially his fault. If he hadn't outlined the sheer stifling boredom of being held in protective custody and— Sheera stopped. He had set her up, she realized suddenly. She had thought there was something slightly odd about the way he had presented the matter. He had made her volunteer. He had wanted her along on this!

But why?

Silence enshrouded them. Damien made no attempt to correct her impression. There was a lot at stake here. Could he draw her in completely? Should he? He had brought her along in case he never found Stanislaus. He knew that he had been hoping against hope that the man would make an eleventh-hour appearance. Now Damien knew it was futile to go on hoping.

Sheera pondered her situation, trying to find some sense in it.

They were served their coffee and the confection Sheera had ordered.

"He's late," she commented, swirling her finger in the tiny bit of powdered sugar that remained on her plate after she had eaten her pastry.

Damien shifted in his seat. "Yes, I know." *Late or dead,* he thought. He could only surmise that Stanislaus had never returned to his quarters, never received the message that had been left for him. Maybe he couldn't receive any more messages. Damien pushed the thought out of his mind. He didn't want to think about it. He had always liked Stanislaus.

That was the trouble with this job. He tended to form attachments, make friendships that might not survive the day. He glanced at Sheera. He had no business involving her in this. It was too dangerous. Yet he had been given no choice. She had turned up at just the right time, an unexpected ace in the hole. Without her, they would have been forced to adopt another plan. What plan, he had no idea.

Well, it was time to get things moving. There was no telling how much time they had left. Bokowski could be closing in on them, if he wasn't watching them this very moment. Damien scanned the street again. Nothing seemed out of the ordinary. But then, that was their gift, making things seem ordinary, lulling suspicions and dulling senses. He could never be too cautious.

He turned to Sheera, who was still absently moving her finger through the light sprinkling of sugar, making patterns on the plate. He remembered what she had felt like against him, remembered the soft curves pressing against his body. *No, don't,* he warned himself. *You've got to keep a clear head. Being sensitive to her vulnerability isn't going to help either of you. She's just someone you're working with, an amateur the gods have whimsically sent your way.* With luck, they both would get out of this alive and he could send her on her way, unscathed.

At least, he hoped so.

It was time to use their ace, he thought.

"Sheera?"

"Hmm?"

"How would you like to go to the ladies' room for me?"

Sheera stared at him.

Chapter Fourteen

"I beg your pardon?" Sheera stared at him, bewildered. She waited for Damien to elaborate. He gave her a perfunctory smile while slowly, methodically, he cast a quick glance in all directions. Something was definitely about to happen. Sheera could feel it. She was developing a sixth sense when it came to Damien.

Apparently satisfied that no one was within hearing range, Damien turned his attention to Sheera. "It's time to let you in on the rest of this."

Sheera's pulse quickened. All her sensory functions became alive with anticipation. Something akin to fear telegraphed through her. Her adrenaline began to flow as an electric intensity took over. Was he serious? Was he finally going to tell her everything? Or was this all going to lead to another dead end?

"Well, go on," she urged.

He drew his coffee cup to his lips and sipped slowly. "I want you to go into the second stall from the right. The second half of the paper is taped to the inside of the tank's lid."

"How did he get into the ladies' room?"

"He didn't. He sent in his wife."

"Oh." That made sense, if any of this did. She felt her courage waning just a little. *This is what you came for, remember? Once this is over, your life will get back to normal, the way it was before.*

She looked at Damien and wondered if she really wanted her life to get back to normal. The answer was a resounding no. But she didn't know what to do about it.

"Ready?" he asked. She shook her head, gathering her scattered thoughts together. He misread her hesitation. "Afraid?"

"I've never been afraid of a bathroom in my life," she quipped nervously.

What was there to be nervous about? Damien was competent and he hadn't seen any agent dogging their tracks. None, she thought, suddenly remembering the plane trip, that he mentioned. She looked at him sharply. "Are we alone?"

"How do you mean that?"

"Is anyone following us?"

This time he answered her seriously. "Not that I know of."

Yes, there was that, too, she thought. Someone could be watching, someone he had no knowledge of. Well, even if he was, she had a right to use the rest room. Why should anyone who was watching be any more suspicious about her entering there than he had been when she had entered the Historical Museum earlier?

"Ready," she said, drawing her courage together.

"All right," he said, his voice expressionless. "In your purse is a bogus document. When you retrieve the one we're after, I want you to slip that one in its place."

"In my purse? There's no document in my purse," she contradicted.

"There is as of this morning."

"Oh, I forgot." Her mouth felt incredibly dry. "You're the one who can make passports appear at will." She had been walking around all morning with something that had been doctored to look like a top-secret document. It was tantamount to having a bomb in her possession without knowing it. It annoyed her to be used like this. But then she relented. He had his reasons, she supposed, giving him the benefit of the doubt.

Damien left a ten-dollar bill that Sheera knew would gladden the heart of the waiter. Nonchalantly, they crossed the narrow street and approached the public rest room.

"I'll wait for you out here," he said, taking a position out on the sidewalk.

"I wouldn't advise your coming in with me," she cracked as she pushed open the heavy door.

She walked out almost immediately.

He looked behind her, half expecting to see someone with a gun. "What's the matter?" he asked.

"It's under repair," she told him.

"The whole rest room?" he cried in frustrated disbelief.

"There are only four stalls," she answered. "There's a maintenance man in there right now."

Damien sighed, perturbed. "Ask him how long it's going to take."

She frowned, feeling foolish. But she walked back in. The door with the out-of-order sign on it was pushed wide open and the sign couldn't be seen until after she walked in. The maintenance man, a thin man of medium height, was dressed in dirty coveralls that were frayed at the cuffs, as if he kept catching them with his heels. He looked surprised to see her again. Surprised and happy. He welcomed any break in his routine.

Sheera faced the mirror and began to wash her hands in the discolored sink. The water ran yellow at first and then only slowly began to clear. Light yellow, Sheera noted, distressed, but she kept the ruse up. Glancing into the mirror, she saw the maintenance man looking at her curiously. He told her that the rest room was closed to the public.

She murmured that she only wanted to wash the city dirt from her hands. Casually, as if only making conversation, she asked him how long his repairs would take. He puffed up his chest importantly and said it all depended on the condition of certain things. He leaned on his mop as he proceeded to outline all that needed to be done. His importance grew with each sentence. It was just the first stall that had the problem, he told her.

Sheera sighed with relief. Then, aware that he was looking at her strangely, she quickly added that it was reassuring to have such dedicated public servants. With that, she hurried out.

The document was still safe, she hoped.

"Well?" Damien asked as she approached him. He actually appeared to be agitated. His agitation generated ambivalent feelings in Sheera. She felt more secure at seeing yet another sign of his being human, but it did shake her faith in him a little. After all, he was the one who was never fazed by anything.

Sheera held her hands before her, to let the wind dry them. Among other things, the rest room was out of paper towels. "I just got a lesson in plumbing," Sheera said. They began to walk away casually.

"And?"

"He told me the location of another public rest room."

"What's the matter with your hands?" he asked, noticing the odd way in which she was holding them up.

"They're wet. I had to do something while I was talking to him," she explained.

"What about this rest room?" Damien pressed. "How long is it going to be out of service?"

She ran her hand over her chin, mimicking the maintenance man. "That all depends, you see, upon the condition of the inner workings of the toilet."

Damien stopped her. "He wasn't fixing—"

"No, not our tank." She couldn't help grinning. "Our tank," she repeated with a nervous laugh. "Sounds kind of romantic."

"I think you had too many of those little cakes at the café," he said dryly.

She gave him a covert look. "I've had too much of something," she said, thinking of the fantasies last night had generated in her mind.

He didn't understand, but let the statement drop. They had to get into that rest room somehow.

"What do we do now?" she asked.

"Go back to the café and order more coffee."

"By the time this is over, I'm going to slosh," she complained, following him.

"Fortunes of the job," he said philosophically.

"Just don't blame me if I'm up all night," she murmured as they sat down again at the same table they had previously occupied.

"Blame you?" he echoed. "I'm counting on it."

She looked at him, smiling. She thought that despite all this, he was still thinking of last night. But her smile faded when she saw the serious look on his face. He was obviously working on an alternate plan. Now what?

The white-aproned waiter looked surprised and pleased to see them back. Sheera told him that she had raved so much about the café's confectionery cakes that her friend decided he wanted to try one, too.

The waiter happily retreated to fetch the pastry.

SEVERAL CUPS OF COFFEE and three pieces of cake later, the maintenance man finally emerged out of the ladies' room. Standing in the square, he dramatically wiped his brow for the benefit of anyone who might be watching. Disappointed that no one paid him any heed, he walked over to his shabby Fiat and dropped his tools into the trunk.

"Now?" Sheera asked, eager to get this over with.

Damien put a hand over hers, pressing against it. "Give it another few minutes," he advised. "We don't want him to see you."

"Why?" She couldn't see what difference it would make.

"He might think it odd that you had a fixation about that particular rest room. We don't want to arouse anyone's suspicions."

No, she certainly didn't want to do that. In a way, she wished that she could enter the public rest room and still somehow remain sitting in her chair.

She watched as the maintenance man took his time packing the remainder of his tools. Rather than carry them out all at once, he made several trips, stretching out the job as long as possible. Another job was probably waiting for him and he was in no hurry to get to it.

Sheera wondered, as she watched, how Damien would have managed if she hadn't come along. Probably would have seduced a local girl into doing it for him, she mused. The improbability of that did not register with as much intensity as the thought of the word "seduced" did. She wondered again if he made a practice of doing that, then decided that in her case, it didn't apply. There had been no mindless seduction last night. She was a big girl now and she knew exactly what she was getting into.

A rather hopeless situation.

"Sheera?" Damien was staring at her oddly. "Are you all right?"

She roused herself. "Yes, why?"

"You had an odd look on your face. You're not freezing up on me, are you?"

"Of course not," she said quickly as her insides began to turn to jelly.

It was time to act. "He's gone."

Sheera looked to where the Fiat had been parked. The space was empty.

Sheera rose. Damien stayed where he was. "You're not coming with me?" she asked. It was an effort for her to keep her voice steady.

"If anyone's watching, it might look a little odd if I accompany you twice to the same facility. I'm afraid you're on your own this time."

"Thanks a lot," she muttered under her breath.

But he heard her. "Don't worry, I'll be right here."

"Safe," she couldn't help saying.

"Never quite that," he countered.

And he was right. Still, he had chosen this way of life. She more or less had it thrust upon her.

The longer she stood and internally philosophized, she told herself, the longer this thing would be drawn out. She marched across the street.

To her surprise, the out-of-order sign was still on the door, which was now closed. "Why, that little weasel. He took all that time and he didn't fix it." She felt momentarily drained. She pushed the door gingerly, trying it on a whim. It gave. He hadn't locked it.

Wishing she could appear as casual as Damien, she pretended to stare at the sign. She hoped her slightly bewildered performance convinced anyone who might be watching that she didn't understand the words. Satisfied that she had waited long enough, Sheera went in.

The unpleasant odors of the public facility immediately assaulted her nose. The tile beneath her feet was a muddy brown, made that way by design and the traffic of countless users. She hurried to the third stall, the one that was second from the end. Locking herself in, she turned to look at the tank. It wasn't where it was supposed to be. All that stood on the floor was the bare bowl with its cracked wooden seat. Where...?

Sheera looked up and realized that the tank was overhead.

Gingerly, she climbed up on the toilet seat, resting her hand on the toilet paper rack for leverage. The paper felt rough and stiff beneath her hand. "No wonder that scientist sold out. I would have defected to the West for the toilet paper alone," she mumbled to herself. Her heart was hammering in her ears and she was cracking lame jokes. *I'm truly going to be certifiably crazy by the time this is all over.*

Summoning all her courage, she struggled to lift the lid off the tank without dropping it. Sweat began to gather along her spine. Sheera tried not to think about the consequences of what she was doing.

She was suddenly very grateful for the out-of-order sign on the door. She couldn't expect a helpful nun to pop up twice in her life, and anyone else walking in would want to know what in the world she was up to.

Hurry up with your job, she urged herself.

Not your job, she amended. *His job. You're just an unwilling accomplice, remember?* Someone who had one whimsical flight of fancy and was now paying for it dearly.

Her arms ached and sweat was beginning to form at the base of her hairline. The lid weighed a ton.

Finally!

Sheera had the lid free and gratefully lowered her arms. Turning it over, she muttered a prayer that the document was still in there and hadn't come loose, to be ruined by the water. The cellophane wrapping could only be counted on to hold out so long. She couldn't bear the idea that all this energy had been spent for nothing.

Not nothing. You have last night.

Precious good last night would do her if they were ever discovered by the KGB, she thought.

It was there!

Carefully, she pulled off the tape and removed the cellophane-wrapped paper from the inside of the lid. She hid the document on her person, knowing that the very act would incriminate her. Again, there was no choice. Sheera hated having no choice, hated being forced into things. But she was in on it now, in for the full count.

She opened her purse. Rifling through it, she found the bogus document Damien had put in. She placed it inside the lid, retaping it carefully.

"Now—" she sighed, looking up overhead "—to put this back."

DAMIEN SAT nursing the remnants of his coffee. The waiter had come by and solicitously asked him if there was anything else he wanted. Damien had just shaken his head.

If the man had offered him more coffee, he thought, he would have strangled him. The coffee was bitter and left a horrid taste in his mouth. Just as did the situation right now.

She hadn't come out.

He watched the ugly squat building across the street, waiting. His instincts told him there was nothing to worry about, at least as far as she was concerned. But he knew his instincts had been dulled after last night. The very fact was unusual. He had had more than his share of women. In his line of work, it would have been difficult not to. Murphy had referred to him on more than one occasion as the agency's international Romeo. Damien had never been content with any woman. They all ran together in his mind now and he had trouble differentiating them. Especially after last night.

Something different had happened last night. Something that surprised him. Something that he had sensed about her all along, from the very first. The closer he got to her, the more he wanted her. There was no crest of satisfaction that followed their union. Another higher plateau kept beckoning. He couldn't get enough of her.

Damn it, where was she?

Had he allowed his feelings to dupe him after all? The agency did have that slight margin of doubt about her. Was there a way out of this bathroom, the way there had been out of the one at the airport?

Code Name: Love

He looked about. The streets were sparsely populated, but still, if she had climbed out, she would have attracted some sort of attention, wouldn't she?

He couldn't be sure.

Poles, he had been briefed, were different from their Russian neighbors, more independent, more prone to challenge rules, even beneath the yoke of communism. Anyone seeing Sheera, other than a police official, might very well look the other way, applauding her bravery at escaping whatever it was that they might surmise she was escaping.

A cooing noise caught his attention. A gray-and-white pigeon had approached him on the ground, exhibiting no signs of fear. He took a crumb from his plate and tossed it to the bird. With a flap of its wings, the bird scurried over to the tidbit and devoured it.

It came back.

Why didn't she come back?

Was he the one who was being a pigeon after all? He had been the one to suggest taking her as insurance, just in case he couldn't contact Stanislaus.

He wondered what had happened to Stanislaus.

What if...?

He saw her coming out of the ladies' room. He couldn't remember when he had been so happy to see anyone in his life. Or so relieved.

"Is that smile for me or...?" She let her voice trail off mischievously.

"Both," he answered. "What went on in there?" he wanted to know.

"Really, Damien, do I quiz you when you go to the men's room?" she sniffed. She ordered another coffee and the waiter brought it out. Now that her mission was finally over, she felt almost giddy in her triumph. She wanted to draw the moment out, just as he had drawn out his explanations. She downed her coffee.

"That's awful," he couldn't help remarking.

"You're right." She replaced the cup in the saucer. "I wish I had something stronger."

"Then you did...?"

Her eyes were sparkling with triumph. A sense of euphoric accomplishment took hold of her. "Yes, I sure did."

He rose, taking her arm. "C'mon. I think it's time to move on."

"Home?" she asked hopefully.

No, that might arouse suspicion if they were being watched. It was best to incorporate this stop into a program of sightseeing. "No, I think I'd like to see the palace."

"Which one?" Sheera asked, flipping open the guidebook. "We've already seen two of them."

"The rest."

Sheera sighed as she followed him.

IT WAS NEARLY FIVE O'CLOCK when Damien finally called an end to their sightseeing excursion.

"So soon?" Sheera asked dryly. "There must be at least two or three blocks in this city we haven't covered yet." She was bone-tired. At the other end of the euphoric high was an exhausted low, and she had reached that point now. They had done what they had set out to do. It was time to retreat and go home. Her real home. Back in Manhattan. Although she felt guilty about deceiving her aunt and about cutting short the first visit they had ever had, she knew she couldn't sleep well, until she was back in her own country.

But could she sleep well without him?

One night does not change an entire lifetime, she told herself stubbornly as she got into the taxi Damien had hailed. Mechanically, she gave the man the address.

No, it might not change an entire lifetime, but it did color the immediate future.

Stop thinking about him and keep your mind clear, she told herself. *You're not out of this yet, not by a long shot.*

HER AUNT WAS HOME and bubbling over with enthusiasm when they walked through the door. "Tell me everything you saw," she instructed before Sheera even had time to take off her coat.

Sheera sank wearily onto the sofa and it sighed along with her as she sank into the single long cushion. "Forgive me, but I'm very, very tired."

"But of course," Aunt Zosia said, giving a nod of her head. "What you need is some good food and then off you go to bed. You still have a different clock inside of you, yes?"

"Clock?"

"I think she means the time change," Damien explained.

Aunt Zosia's nodding smile told him he had guessed correctly.

"Not a bad idea, Sheera," Damien agreed.

For a moment, she thought he meant "bed" the way she had thought of it several hours ago. But a closer scrutiny of his face told her that she was wrong. Something else was on his mind.

Chapter Fifteen

"Oh, please, just five more minutes," Sheera groaned sleepily.

"Soon, Sheera, soon you can go back to sleep," Damien promised, whispering against her ear.

It was close to ten o'clock. He had wanted some time to lapse after they came into the bedroom. Damien wanted to be sure that Aunt Zosia was asleep before Sheera began working with the document. While waiting, Sheera had fallen asleep, leaning against Damien's chest. His arm had gone numb cradling her against him. When the time came, he had felt almost reluctant to wake her. She looked so serene, so overwhelmingly beautiful.

That wouldn't look too good on his report, he thought dryly: "Postponed wrapping up mission because interpreter was too beautiful to wake." He grinned to himself. Wouldn't Bascom blow a gasket! Damien sobered. He was getting a little punchy. It was time to get all this over with. Gently, he shook her shoulder.

Sheera stirred, a sleep-drugged protest on her lips. He tried again.

"Sheera, wake up," he implored softly.

Sheera opened her eyes. For a moment, she was totally disoriented. Damien's face was the first thing she focused on. Had they— No, they hadn't. She glanced down. She was still fully clothed, still wearing the same pale yellow shirtwaist dress. Things began falling into place. She remembered the public rest room, the exchange, the weight of the tank lid.

Sheera rubbed her eyes and struggled into an upright sitting position. She made him think of a small child.

Damien grinned to himself. That was no small child he had held in his arms last night. That was the most arousing, most desirable woman he had ever had the fortune to encounter.

"I must have fallen asleep," she murmured, stretching.

He watched the way she moved. Desire flared in him, but he snuffed it out. "Must have," he agreed. "Where's the document, Sheera?"

"The document?" For a moment, her brain went numb. What had she...? Oh, yes. The itchy feeling against her abdomen. "Oh, right." She saw relief wash away the sudden worried look in his eyes. "I've got it right here." She unbuttoned the top of her dress and reached inside. Damien watched in silence, picturing his hands there instead of hers.

"Need any help?" he offered.

"I thought your mind was on your work," she teased, now fully awake.

"All work and no play makes Damien a dull boy," he countered with a wink.

She handed him the document. "One thing no one can ever accuse you of is being dull."

"Thank you." She saw a twinkle come into his eyes.

"Don't thank me. I have nothing to do with it," she said glibly.

"Oh," he said as he glanced down at the document, "I wouldn't say that."

She wanted to ask him what he meant by that but knew that his mind was elsewhere now. He had turned into the well-trained professional right before her eyes. The twinkle had changed into an excited, expectant gleam.

The document was unharmed. He placed it down in front of him on the bed like a revered vessel.

"All right, Sheera, do your thing."

While she studied it, Damien took his suitcase out of the closet. Pushing his clothes aside, he pulled out his pad and pen.

"It looks like gibberish."

He turned and looked up sharply. "What?"

"It looks like gibberish," she repeated. She tucked her long legs under her, trying to make herself more comfortable on the bed.

"You can't read it?" The words came out slowly, dressed in disbelief.

She turned the document around. "Yes," she told him, "and no."

He sat down on the bed, next to her. "At least you left out 'maybe.'" His mind began to race, trying to think of an alternative.

She looked at him, then back at the paper in her hand. "That, too."

Damien's brow furrowed. This really put a major snag in things. He had been chosen for the mission for one qualification and one qualification only. He had the ability to memorize things almost instantly, recalling them at will. But first he had to be able to read what he was going to be memorizing. He couldn't commit something in a foreign tongue to memory. He had tried more than once and failed. There had to be a grain of comprehension associated with what he was memorizing. Having looked over the paper, he knew that he had nothing to go on here without a translation.

"You really can't read it?" he asked again, hoping against hope for a different answer this time.

"Oh, I can read it," Sheera was quick to say, still looking at the paper. She missed the look of bewilderment that crossed his features. "What I mean is that I don't understand it."

He sighed, letting himself fall flat on his back, his head landing neatly in her lap as she raised the document up, out of the way.

"You're not supposed to understand it," he said laughing, as a rush of euphoric relief washed over him. It was going to be all right. "*I'm* not supposed to, either. It's a scientific paper. A theoretical presentation. Even most doctorates in physics would have a hard time understanding it. Unless you've got a Ph.D. in physics—" He eyed her playfully from his upside-down position.

"I don't."

"Then you wouldn't be able to make real sense out of it. I just need the words in between the configurations translated." He sat up, propping himself on his elbow, his face turning deadly serious. "Can you do it?"

Sheera squared her shoulders, spiking her hair with her fingers and pushing it over her shoulder. She pulled the pad he had taken out on her lap. "This isn't going to be easy," she declared.

He sighed inwardly. She was up to it, thank God. "It never is."

She made a face at him. "Too bad they've done away with *Poor Richard's Almanac*," she said dryly. "You could have made a real killing with them."

"Please—" he held up his hands as if he were trying physically to block the words from reaching him "—don't mention killing in my presence," he teased.

Sheera laughed softly. It broke the tension that hung in the air. She got down to work.

"HERE, I THINK THIS IS IT," she said finally, passing the pad to him. "It's rather difficult to translate words you're unfamiliar with," she complained wearily.

Damien hid his impatience from her. The sooner they got rid of the evidence, the better off they would both be. He still wished that Stanislaus had turned up. Feeling what he did for Sheera, he still would have preferred Stanislaus to have done the actual translating. It wasn't that Damien didn't trust Sheera. He did. He had gone too far not to. But Stanislaus was an expert at his job. And she, she was just an innocent bystander.

A very intelligent bystander, he amended, recalling the dossier Bascom had given him on her. The department was extremely thorough when it wanted to be. Nothing about her had been left unexplored. He had been given her full background, had been told of her academic accomplishments and her meteoric rise in her career. If Stanislaus couldn't be located, then she was an admirable substitute.

He took the pad from her.

Sheera massaged the bridge of her nose, fanning her fingers out lightly to include the tear ducts on either side. Her eyes hurt. She had concentrated so hard, she felt as if her head was about to explode. The light in the room was from a single lamp on the bureau. It was dim, and the author of this paper had writing somewhat akin to chicken scratchings. The man who had written it might have been brilliant, but he had lousy handwriting, she thought grudgingly.

She opened her eyes and looked at Damien. He had long since taken off his jacket and the sleeves of his powder-blue shirt were rolled up. Every muscle in his body appeared to be concentrating. She watched his face, fascinated. She was almost able to see the words being drawn from the page into his brain. He spent a long time poring over it.

Damien closed his eyes for a moment, mentally reciting everything he had just read. Opening his eyes again, he looked at the sheet in his hand.

Perfect. He had it.

Sheera watched apprehensively as he took out a match and then lit her translation. "Are you sure you have it memorized already?" she asked incredulously. "I don't want to go through that again."

"I'm sure." There was no doubt whatsoever in his voice.

The blue-and-yellow flame almost hypnotized her as she stared at it. When the paper had burned down to a tiny shred, the flame coming unbearably close to his fingers, Damien blew it out. The scorched remnant was crumpled between his fingertips.

"You'll burn yourself," Sheera cried, then lowered her voice again, looking over her shoulder. She half expected her aunt to come running in.

But no one came. Sheera sighed, giving Damien a sheepish look.

"Better to burn my fingers than us," he said philosophically. He began to repeat the procedure with the actual document, then stopped. He held the second burning match in his hand, then looked at Sheera. "Are you absolutely sure?"

The thought that this was probably the most important question she had ever been asked floated through her mind. She nodded. "I'm sure."

Flame met paper and soon, the second half of the sought-after document existed only in Damien's head.

Sheera rocked back on her heels, relaxing. She hadn't realized how tense she actually was until she looked down and saw that she was gripping a piece of the bedspread in her hands, kneading it with her fingers as the flame had gotten smaller and smaller.

She dropped the wrinkled section self-consciously and took Damien's hand instead. Turning its palm upward, she examined it. "You're hurt." His fingertips were slightly charred.

"I've been worse." He shrugged off her concern.

"Really?"

She couldn't imagine anything harming him. She didn't even want to think of him having been hurt. But something pressed her to ask. *If you're to love him, you have to face knowing certain things about him*. The fact that there was no future in all of this was pushed aside for the moment. "Can you tell me about it?" she asked.

"Only in vague, general terms," he answered honestly.

She understood his reasons, but she didn't have to like them. His job was an entity that would always come between them, just as certainly as it had brought them together. "This job of yours isn't high on trust, is it?"

"On the contrary, it's very high on trust, trust that nothing is as it seems." He smiled. "And then, there's trusting your instincts. The way I trusted mine about you."

"Oh?" she asked archly. She hadn't felt that he trusted her, not until the past few minutes. "Tell me about that."

"Your very pretty hands hold my life in them," he said, taking them to his lips and kissing each individually. Now that the formula was his, he could turn his mind to other things.

Sheera felt a shiver travel along her spine with each sensuous kiss. His kisses felt as intimate as if they had touched the most private part of her being.

"How?" she breathed, wanting to hear more. Wanting to feel more.

He released her hands and, very lightly, opened another button on her dress. "You could have been a very clever spy, totally unknown to our side. You could have turned me over to the authorities at any time."

He kissed the hollow of her throat and slowly moved to her collarbone. He undid the last two buttons. His kisses trailed down to the tempting valley between her breasts. Sheera could feel her heart hammering as she tried to carry on a semblance of coherent conversation. "You were with me all the time."

"With you," he agreed, "but who knows what you could have said to the butcher?" The dress left one shoulder. "Or the taxi driver?" It slipped from the other shoulder. "Or the maintenance man?"

Her bra with its front clasp hung to either side of her breasts. He covered them with his hands, gently massaging, his thumbs rubbing against the tips, which hardened instantly at the very first touch.

"I felt like a babe in the woods here," Damien told her. He lowered his head, kissing the supple flesh that he held in his hands.

Sheera moaned lightly as she wrapped her arms around his head and cradled him closer. "A very, very capable babe," she managed to answer.

"One who relies totally on your pure heart." She felt the words ripple against her bare skin. Suddenly, he drew back. "Teach me how to say 'let's go to bed.'"

"Planning on becoming a Polish Romeo?" she asked wryly.

"Only yours. C'mon," he teased. "I'm a fast study."

"That—" she laughed "—you don't have to tell me. Okay, but the Poles are romantic souls, so the invitation is far more subtle in their language. Listen carefully." She said the phrase slowly.

To her surprise, he got it right on the very first try. And hearing him say it stirred her even more. The flame within her rose far higher than any that had burned in the room before. She let him ease her back down onto the bed, the length of his body curving against hers.

"Do you know," Damien asked, releasing the hook that held her wraparound dress together, "that you're beautiful when you translate?"

Despite the heat of the moment, a laugh bubbled in her throat. "No one's ever said that to me before." *No one's done a lot of things you do to me,* she added silently, her eyes glowing warmly as she watched him in the dim light, her emotions raging within her.

"They should have," he whispered. "You are. Beautiful when you're fleeing, too. I don't think I've ever before seen anyone quite so beautiful as you."

How she wished with her whole heart and soul that she could believe him. But he was talking in the excitement of the moment, she told herself, heady with the triumph of a mission nearly perfectly executed.

Wrong word, she realized and gulped.

A mission perfectly carried out. Tomorrow, they would be on their way home. He to his and she to hers. The thought filled her with a desperate, overwhelming sorrow.

But she had tonight. She still had tonight, she thought, clinging to that reality. And she was going to use it to the best of her ability. The memory of their lovemaking was going to have to last her a long, long time.

"I bet you say that to all the women who fish secret documents out of public bathrooms for you."

"Oddly enough—" he ran a finger down between her breasts, the very action teasing her into anticipation "—you're the first."

"The first what?" To her satisfaction, her tone didn't reveal how important his answer was to her. "The first to fish something out of a public bathroom in Warsaw for you?" He was driving her crazy, she thought, wanting to stay his hand and yet wanting to press it closer at the same time.

"Just the first," he answered just before he kissed her.

The kiss exploded any pretense she might have wanted to cling to for the sake of preserving her pride once the morning light came. It would be impossible for him, she thought, not to realize just how his kiss affected her. How *he* affected her. Her lips clung to his hungrily.

She felt his hands caressing her body, passing along her hips and drawing away the last shred of clothing. She burned for him.

"Take yours off now," she asked, tugging unsuccessfully at his shirt. "Or do you plan to make love to me formally?"

"Formally, informally, in any way you want, just so long as it happens."

It was happening now, she thought as she freed the buttons from their holes. He lay back, content to let her do the work.

"Help me," she instructed. "You're not much of a gentleman."

She wanted to undress him quickly because she felt as if she were about to explode with desire. And also because, despite her passion and the fact that they had made love the night before, she still felt a bit awkward being nude while he was dressed.

"On the contrary, I wouldn't dream of insulting your capabilities," he answered, a smile of repressed yearning on his face. "You're a modern woman. Show me what you know."

"Not very much." The words had slipped out innocently, and she knew immediately that she'd made a mistake. Her admission had stripped her of her shield. But she wanted him to know that her involvement with him was special to her, that she didn't have casual lovers.

He guided her hands back to their task. "You could have fooled me."

"What I know," Sheera said, raising her head and trying to hold on to just a shred of pride, "comes by instinct." Quickly, without thinking about what she was doing, she pulled the belt out of its catch, then unhooked his trousers.

"You have wonderful, wonderful instincts," he assured, taking her swiftly moving hands and pressing them closer to his body. "But you need to work on your timing. Timing, Sheera," he whispered softly, "is everything."

Code Name: Love

He was melting her again, she thought.

Any poise she was trying to maintain was fading. What did it matter if he knew how much she cared? For the sake of her pride? Pride was a cold, empty word that had nothing to do with what she was feeling at that moment. Pride was something she could feel when she looked at a job well done. The emotion he aroused in her was something entirely different. It had nothing to do with pride. Love seldom did.

He lifted his hips for her. "Is there no one else?"

"In the room? Not that I see," she said, trying to force a laugh, but failing. Damn her repression. Why was it so hard for her to put her feelings in words?

Because you're afraid, more afraid of being hurt than you are of what could have happened to you this afternoon.

"In your life, Sheera." He switched positions with her. Now she was on the bed and he was looming over her, blocking out everything else. "Is there no one else in your life?"

"No." The word was barely audible.

"Truth?"

"Truth," she repeated. "I don't make a habit of sleeping with men—especially not with two at the same time." The words were coming out all wrong.

But he knew what she meant. She felt his smile filter into her being. "Gets a little crowded that way, I've heard."

"Just heard?" she asked. Since he was asking her questions, she needed to have answers to some of her own.

"Just heard," he confirmed. "Never been in bed with another man."

He was laughing at her. She frowned and he smoothed back the tightening muscles in her brow until she was forced to smile at him. "That's not what I meant," she protested. "Have you ever...?"

"No," he whispered against her lips, "never."

She thought she heard him add, "Not like this," but she wasn't sure if it was his voice or her own mind that had added the postscript. All she knew was that she was suddenly far too consumed with longing to go on talking any longer.

And so was he.

Chapter Sixteen

It was particularly chilly the following morning. Sheera sat at the tiny kitchen table, warming her hands on a steaming cup of tea. Her knees were touching Damien's, who sat adjacent to her, but for the moment, it was her aunt who occupied her mind.

"So soon?" Aunt Zosia's deep voice was mournful as she prepared breakfast.

"I'm afraid so," Sheera said into her teacup. "I have this tight schedule, you see." She avoided looking at her aunt, afraid that guilt would be evident in her eyes.

Think how much worse you'd feel if something happened to her because of all this, Sheera thought. The need to leave was urgent. Damien had assured her, when she had questioned him about it, that because they had destroyed all the evidence, her aunt could not be implicated in anything. But Sheera was still worried.

"Yes, yes, I understand," Aunt Zosia sighed, bringing over an old, battered pot to the table. Using a thick wooden ladle, she began doling out a large portion of oatmeal. Sheera tried not to wince as she watched it ooze into her bowl like a lethargic snail crawling down the side. "But I do not have to like it."

"Neither do I," Sheera said, cringing as she looked at the oatmeal.

"Maybe business will bring us by this way again."

Damien's words severed Sheera's unholy communion with her breakfast. She looked at him, aghast. Was he serious? Were they coming back again for some reason? What hadn't he told her?

"That would be nice." Aunt Zosia enforced her agreement with a sharp nod of her head. A broad smile captured her lips. "That would be very nice." An even healthier serving of oatmeal found its way into Damien's bowl. Aunt Zosia returned the ladle to the pot and patted Sheera's shoulder. "You have made the right choice with him," she pronounced authoritatively.

Sheera offered her aunt a bright smile. *If you only knew,* she thought.

There was a sharp rap on the door.

"Now who could be disturbing us at this hour?" Aunt Zosia complained. She put the pot on the stove burner with a heavy thud, then wiped her hands on her apron as she crossed the few steps to the door.

"Andrzej!"

The inflection in her aunt's voice made the name sound like a curse.

"Andrzej" was a wide, hulking man with fleshy lips and a nose that seemed almost incomplete because of the way it turned up at the end. He stood in the doorway for a moment, his huge frame filling it almost entirely. He appeared even larger than he was because he was wearing an obviously expensive fur coat and hat.

He didn't wait for an invitation. Instead, he walked into the apartment as if he owned it. He looked out of place in the shabby apartment.

"I did not ask you in," Aunt Zosia said pointedly, still holding the door open.

"But you meant to," Andrzej said, taking off his hat. His sparse, slicked-down black hair barely covered his balding pate.

He was speaking to Aunt Zosia, but his attention was focused on the two seated at the table. His deep-set eyes seemed to take in everything about them in an instant, leaving nothing unnoticed. He took Sheera's hand in his, his body assuming a formal stance. There was something discomforting about the soft flesh that captured hers.

"It is a pleasure to meet you, Sheera O'Malley."

Sheera looked at Damien a little apprehensively as Andrzej bent over her hand and kissed it.

Damien moved his head from side to side, ever so slightly. A look of warning came into his eyes.

"I would say the same," Sheera answered, finding her voice, "if I knew who you were."

Aunt Zosia, vexed, cleared her throat, "It would be better if you did not know," she said.

Andrzej straightened up, still holding Sheera's hand. She longed to pull it free, but she left it where it was, sandwiched between two beefy paws. Trapped. Sheera hoped she wouldn't start to perspire.

"Now, Zosiu," the man chided.

A look of resignation creased Aunt Zosia's brow. "This is Andrzej Pulaski. He is the local government offical here." Aunt Zosia fairly spat out the words.

Andrzej chuckled, stroking Sheera's hand. The sensation of being trapped seeped further into her consciousness. She fought to keep her breathing regular. "Your obedient servant, Zosiu." The piglike eyes twinkled as they looked at the older woman.

"Not mine." She made no effort to hide her contempt for the man. Sheera was surprised that her aunt was so outspoken against a government official and that the man took it all as a joke. Was she worrying for nothing?

"It is just her way of denying her feelings. But by and by, she will give in to me," he said knowingly.

"Not before I'm dead and gone," Aunt Zosia declared vehemently in Polish. She crossed her arms before her chest, looking like a forbidding fortress not to be breeched.

Andrzej's attention shifted to Damien. Sheera could see his expression change. Maybe she was just too nervous, too suspicious. But the look in Andrzej's eyes and the expression on his face telegraphed a knowing suspicion.

"And you are Damien Conrad."

Damien half rose in his seat, taking Andrzej's hand and shaking it heartily. "Yes, I am," he said respectfully. His face remained expressionless. Sheera applauded him.

"Such a strange custom you Americans have, marrying and keeping your names separate, if not your bodies." Andrzej eyed Damien carefully.

"It's called independence," Sheera said, then wished she had not been so quick to answer. *Careful, Sheera,* she warned herself. *This isn't some man you're talking to over cocktails at some Manhattan party*. It wouldn't do to sound as if she were challenging him. It wouldn't do for any of their sakes. What was he doing here? Why now, just when they were leaving? Was it merely a coincidence, or was it something more? She had thought that they had lost the agent at the airport. Everything had been going so well until now. She was worried for all of them, including her aunt.

A knot tightened in Sheera's stomach, as unmanageable as one formed out of wet hemp.

He sat down at the table without being invited and faced Sheera squarely. She felt as if his eyes were probing her mind. "Ah, yes, independence, the word you Americans cherish so much." His lower lip curled slightly in veiled contempt. "Too much independence leads to nothing but chaos. We Poles like order."

"Do not speak for me," Aunt Zosia said, coming up behind Sheera. She placed two protective hands on Sheera's shoulders. "I think that what Sheera does is admirable."

Andrzej shrugged carelessly. "You are only a foolish woman."

"Not so foolish as to accept your proposal," Aunt Zosia retorted smugly.

Sheera expected the florid face to dissolve into a scowl. Instead, the jowls lent themselves to a tolerant smile. "That makes you all the more foolish. But it is only a matter of time. Women have these silly games," he confided to Damien, leaning in his direction. "They like to be courted. So I come," he said, hitting his chest, "pay my respects, prove I am good husband material."

He made his appearance there sound so innocent, Sheera thought. Maybe too innocent. The knot in her stomach was tightening.

"Well, I do not wish to disturb your breakfast," he said, rising.

"That you already have done," Aunt Zosia snapped.

"I will see you again soon, Zosiu," he said, touching her cheek with the tips of his gloves. Aunt Zosia jerked her head back. "And you?" He left the sentence incomplete as he looked from Damien to Sheera.

"I'm afraid we're leaving this morning," Damien said, the proper note of contrition in his voice.

Andrzej appeared to consider Damien's words thoughtfully. "A pity. I had thought that perhaps I could show you around the city."

"Maybe next time," Sheera interjected quickly.

He looked mildly surprised. "You are coming back?"

"Oh, yes," Sheera answered. "Soon. Very soon." Anything to avoid suspicion and make the man leave.

"That is good news," Andrzej said, a broad wink accompanying his words. "Perhaps the next time you come, you can attend our wedding."

Aunt Zosia said nothing, but merely scowled and turned her back toward him. Andrzej took his leave formally. The air became less oppressive as soon as the door shut behind him.

Sheera looked at Damien apprehensively. But as usual, he wore his placid poker face. His eyes were expressionless. The perfect blue mirrors reflected nothing at all. She had learned by now that there was an inverse relationship between his outward concern and the gravity of the situation. She became worried.

"Stupid man," Aunt Zosia muttered, glaring at the closed door. "He has been after me like a dog sniffing out a bone ever since he came to our neighborhood a year ago."

Maybe it was all harmless after all, Sheera thought. Maybe the man was just trying to score a few points with Aunt Zosia by being nice to her niece. He did look about her aunt's age. Maybe he was just taken with her spirit.

Sheera drained her tea, trying to still her frayed nerves.

"He certainly doesn't take a hint," Damien observed. He stood up and walked over to the window.

Aunt Zosia didn't understand the expression and let it pass. Instead, her concern shifted to the bowls on the table. "You did not eat," she accused.

"Not that it wasn't good," Damien said, kissing the woman's forehead quickly, "but—"

"Yes, I know," Aunt Zosia waved away his apology. "He makes me lose my appetite, too." She sighed. "I wish they would transfer him."

"Don't you think it's a little dangerous?" Sheera asked her aunt as she went to join Damien, "to treat him so contemptuously?"

Aunt Zosia looked at her blankly and Sheera repeated herself in Polish. The older woman laughed. "He is used to it. No one likes him. Besides, at my age, what could he do to me?"

"He might force you to marry him," Damien teased.

A strange, vengeful smile spread out over her lips. "He would be very sorry."

They all laughed, then Damien ushered Sheera into the bedroom to get their things. They were already packed. That had been taken care of first thing that morning. Well, Sheera thought smiling fondly at the remembrance, her tension breaking for a moment, not the *very* first thing.

"What do you think?" Sheera asked Damien in a hushed whisper.

"I don't know," he said honestly. "He might just be an overbearing suitor." He gave her hand a reassuring squeeze just before he picked up the luggage. "In any case, let's hope so. Our luck's been good up to now."

"That's what has me worried," she confessed.

"Are you always this optimistic?"

"Only in your company."

"Very flattering." He knew her well enough by now to realize that her light words covered her anxiety. He gave her a reassuring kiss and led the way out.

Sheera hesitated for one second, giving her aunt's bed one last look. That had been the site of her awakening, the site of her blossoming into fulfilled womanhood. She would always remember it with bittersweet memories.

"Are you coming?" Damien asked, poking his head into the room.

"Yes, I was just looking around to make sure we haven't left anything behind," she said quickly, too embarrassed to admit the truth.

"There's not much room to leave it in," he pointed out.

Damn him, he looked as if he could read her mind. Served her right for falling for a spy. It was their job to second-guess everyone.

Aunt Zosia's eyes were damp as she stood by the door watching them. "I will not go with you to the airport," she announced, her hands closing and opening within the apron pockets. "It will seem less like good-bye if I only see you walk out the door." She paused a moment as her voice threatened to break. "This way, I can hope to see you walk through it again."

She embraced her niece, and then Damien, and then spread out an arm to both, hugging them to her. "Take good care of each other," she ordered. "Love is the most important thing in this world. Everything else takes second place."

Sheera nodded, her own eyes beginning to sting. "I wish I could stay a while longer."

"No." Aunt Zosia shook her head. "I think it best that you leave now."

Her words brought a degree of uncertainty to Sheera. Did her aunt suspect anything? "Why do you—?"

"Shh." Aunt Zosia put her finger to her lips. "No questions. Perhaps I am not everything I seem to be, too. And then—" she winked "—perhaps I am."

Too. She had said "too," Sheera thought as they walked out of the tiny apartment. Somehow, her aunt knew.

Maybe it was just a matter of the woman trying to make herself seem important, Sheera argued. No, her aunt wasn't the type.

"Let's hurry," Sheera said to Damien as they walked down the steps to the street. She looked around for a taxi. Their flight wasn't due for several hours, but the sooner they were at the airport, the better she would feel. They would be that much closer to the plane and freedom.

"Permit me to offer you the services of my car."

Sheera turned around with a jerk. Andrzej Pulaski had come up behind them. The smile on his face was icy. As icy as her fingertips.

"THIS ISN'T THE WAY to the airport," Sheera heard herself protest. When Andrzej's official chauffeured car had pulled up alongside them, they had had no choice but to get in. Breaking away and running was out of the question. They would only have been stopped at the airport as they tried to leave. And retaliatory measures might be taken against her aunt.

"No, it is not."

Andrzej rested a hand on her knee. Sheera's immediate reaction was to want to scream, but the look in Damien's eyes warned her not to.

"I don't think my aunt would approve of your familiarity," Sheera managed to say, lifting the man's hand and placing it on his own knee.

Andrzej laughed. "I see this perversely stubborn streak runs in your family." He turned to her, his eyes no longer smiling. A malevolent look had entered them, distorting his features even further.

Sheera thought that never in her life had she seen such an ugly man. Abstractly, she wondered if she would ever have another opportunity.

"We will see how stubborn you remain after a few hours." The voice was mild, but the threat was clear.

"Would you mind telling us what this is all about?" Damien's voice was still polite, still respectful, but Sheera thought she detected a note of steel in it.

"Of course not. It is about our mutual friends, Wawelski," Andrzej said, mentioning the scientist, "and Stanislaus."

It took everything Damien possessed not to change his mildly curious expression. He had been right. They had the interpreter.

"Stanislaus?" he asked, feigning confusion.

"Come, come, no theatrics. I know all about you." Fat fingertips met in a point as he steepled his hands.

How inappropriate, Sheera thought, trying to keep her hatred from showing. He looked as if he were about to pray. Last rites? Sheera thought suddenly.

"Your Mr. Kopeczny told us quite a bit before he inconveniently picked his time to die."

Sheera covered her mouth with her hand, horror flashing across her face. *Don't scream. It's all a ruse.*

This isn't happening. He's just trying to unnerve you. Damn it, why didn't Damien look as if the words had penetrated? He looked as if the hateful man who sat between them like a giant mushroom was just reciting selections from the *TV Guide*. Didn't he have any feelings? Any nerves?

"I'm afraid I still don't understand," Damien protested, shaking his head.

"Come, come, Mr. Conrad," Andrzej said, losing patience. "We are both too old to play such childish games. Just tell us where the document is and you can go free."

Free. The word had never sounded so wonderful, so unattainable, Sheera thought desperately.

Wait a minute! Andrzej was asking him where the document *was*. That meant they hadn't followed them yesterday. They didn't know that she had switched the two! It would be an easy matter just to tell them where the "document" was hidden and— No, she realized, it wasn't. It wasn't an easy matter at all. If Damien freely told them where to find it, Andrzej would be suspicious. They were in for an awful time. Sheera groaned inwardly, trying to steel herself for whatever it was that was coming.

"I really don't have the faintest idea what you're talking about," Damien insisted. "Now, my wife has an important meeting in West Germany to get to and we would really appreciate—"

Andrzej shook his head, pretending to be tolerant. The way he held his hands on his knees, knuckles growing white, told Sheera that his patience was in short supply.

"We would all appreciate different things, my friend. Well, we shall see if we cannot convince you to be more helpful." He picked up a strand of Sheera's hair, bringing it closer and inhaling deeply. "Ah, perfume." His smile was absolutely bone-chilling. "It would be a pity to have you go the way your friend did. It was not a pretty sight."

Sheera began to recite every prayer she had ever learned as a child—in two languages.

THE SLEEK BLACK CAR pulled up silently in front of a drab gray building that flew its Polish flag proudly. Burly guards in uniform stood at the double doors that Andrzej hustled them through. Sheera couldn't even get a good look at any of the people in the hall as he rushed them to their destination.

Not their final one, she hoped.

"Why so quick?" Damien asked, still sounding as if he was being given an unofficial tour of lesser-known parts of Warsaw.

"I have a pressing engagement tonight. I would like this to be all over by then."

What did he mean by "over," Sheera wondered desperately. She looked to Damien for reassurance. But Damien, she could see, was preoccupied. With a plan for their escape, she hoped.

The room Andrzej had brought them into was tremendous, although sparsely furnished. It made Sheera feel small and almost insignificant. She knew it was supposed to. She clung to her spirit, telling herself that they wouldn't be in any danger, that she had to trust Damien to manage somehow to get them out of all this.

But she saw no way.

"Now," Andrzej said, removing his coat and handing it to a thin young man who appeared silently next to him and then disppeared through a door in the back, "shall we try this one more time? Where is the document?"

Damien shook his head. "I'm afraid—"

"No," Andrzej said, "you are not afraid. But you will be."

The severest-looking woman Sheera had ever seen entered the room, through the same door that the thin young man had used. She was followed by a man who easily towered over Damien. And Damien was over six feet tall.

"Take them," Andrzej ordered.

Sheera looked at Damien in mounting fear. "Where are you taking us?" Sheera demanded when Damien said nothing. He might be used to this, but she wanted to know what was going on.

"Perhaps I have made a mistake," Andrzej said complacently, flipping open a long black box on his desk. Instead of cigars, it housed an assortment of chocolates. "Perhaps you already have the document. In any event, we shall find that out soon enough." He popped several chocolates into his mouth.

An awful premonition swept over Sheera.

They were herded out, then separated. The unsmiling, shapeless woman in brown took Sheera to a box-like room. A small barred window provided the only light until the woman switched on an overhead lamp. She motioned at Sheera's clothes.

"I will not!" Sheera cried in Polish, knowing that it was useless to protest but feeling that, for the sake of her trembling nerves, she had to.

Rough hands seized her camel-hair jacket and yanked it off, then grabbed for her lavender blouse.

"All right," Sheera snapped. "I'll do it."

HALF AN HOUR LATER, she found herself deposited back in the cold, unheated room. Damien was already there. Their suitcases, stood open and their clothes were strewn in a mingled heap to one side. The suitcases had been sliced open in every conceivable manner.

No one else was in the room.

Damien took her into his arms quickly. "Are you all right?"

It was the first demonstration of concern he had displayed since the whole interrogation had started. She knew it had to be this way, but she was resentful nonetheless.

"No, I am *not* all right," she snapped, pushing her hair out of her eyes. "I've just been through the most humiliating experience in my life. Do you know where they thought I had that damn document?" she cried, fury and fear filling her voice.

"I can guess," he answered sympathetically.

Sheera trembled, moving her hands up and down her arms to ward off the awful feeling that ran through her. She was fighting the urge to throw up just as hard as she was struggling to keep her courage up.

"I'll make it up to you," he promised.

"Damn right you will," she retorted. "When we get back—*if* we get back—I'm going to pay you back for this."

He pulled her roughly to him, then began stroking her hair, trying to calm her. But he let her talk, knowing she needed to vent her feelings. He just hoped that she wouldn't say the wrong thing.

Sheera's eyes fell on the suitcases. "Oh, God," she wailed, dropping to her knees. "Look what they did." The assault on her possessions made her almost as indignant as the body search had. How dared they! How *dared* they!

"I was always fond of this suitcase," she lamented, trying to pull the shattered case together and then giving up. "My dad got it for me at Gimbels just when I was starting out."

Damien put his hands on her shoulders, bringing her to her feet. "I'll buy you another."

She tried to get hold of herself. "I don't think either one of us is going shopping at Gimbels in the immediate future. I don't think either one of us *has* an immediate future." She turned, searching Damien's face for reassurance. "It's bad, isn't it?" The words were choked out.

"Maybe not."

"You can lie better than that," she mumbled, looking away. But he wouldn't let go of her arms. She looked at him again, wondering why he was clutching her in that way. She tried to pick up a sign, some clues. Instead, she got confused.

"I wish this was over," she muttered.

He agreed with her. "If only we had been given a chance to get to secure the document and pass it on."

Sheera started, then realized what he was after. "Maybe they'll let us go," she said, shaking him free and beginning to pace about the room. Was it bugged? Was there a hidden camera? Oh, God, had there been a camera somewhere when that awful woman had made her strip?

No, don't think about that now. Later, much later. A hundred years from now.

"We could still get to that public rest room and—"
"Quiet!" Damien ordered sharply.
"But—?"

"Don't say anything!"

Sheera jumped, even more perplexed. Had she misunderstood. Didn't he want...? "Who the hell do you think you're yelling at?" she demanded, her anger rising. "I wouldn't be in this mess if it weren't for you."

Just then, Andrzej walked into the room. He was smiling. He had the smile, Sheera couldn't help thinking, of an executioner.

Chapter Seventeen

"By all means, Mr. Conrad, let your wife speak." Andrzej was talking to Damien, but his eyes were on Sheera.

Sheera looked at Damien, waiting for a sign. What was she supposed to do? *Was* she supposed to do anything? Damien's face remained impassive. Only his clenched hands gave a hint as to what he was feeling.

"She has nothing to say," Damien told Andrzej.

Sheera's heart was pounding unevenly. Was this a game of cat and mouse? Was she the bait? What was going on? She roundly cursed the day she had ever followed him.

"No?" Andrzej began to walk slowly around Sheera, studying her from all angles. Sheera thought she was going to lose what little composure she had left. He returned to face her with an evil smile on his face. "Then perhaps you do?" he suggested.

Damien made no answer.

"We'll see. Janie!" he roared over his shoulder.

The door behind them opened and the man who had kidnapped Sheera from her office walked in. Sheera's heart stopped.

Why wasn't Damien talking, Sheera wondered frantically. What was the man going to do to him?

Jan seized her wrist.

Sheera's eyes grew wide as she tried to pull her hand free. She felt as if it had been caught in a steel trap.

What was he going to do to her?

"Damien?" she cried uncertainly.

Damien merely looked at Andrzej, his expression blank.

She was going to be sacrificed. She didn't know why, or what this was about anymore, but she was going to be the sacrificial lamb.

No, no, Damien wouldn't let them do that to her. He wouldn't. He has something up his sleeve. Oh, please, let him have something up his sleeve, she thought desperately.

"She's a very beautiful woman," Andrzej said to Damien, stroking her hair. The movement turned vicious as he snatched a handful of hair, yanking her head back toward him. "It would be a pity," he went on as if nothing had happened, "to change all that."

Sheera felt as if the hairs in the center of her head were being ripped out. She looked to Damien again, hoping against hope to make some sense of this. Why was he putting her through this? How convincing did she have to be in her terror before he said something? Did he want her to blurt it out?

And how long did she have before Jan began his handiwork?

"Still stubborn?" Andrzej asked mildly. A slight nod of his head and a knife appeared in Jan's hand. "Well, then—"

"No!" Damien cried.

Sheera felt dizzy. As she pitched forward, she was aware that Damien caught her. She struggled with her senses. This was no time to faint. She might never wake up again. She had to stay conscious!

"I'll tell you where it is." Damien's voice vaguely penetrated the cloud that was dulling her brain. Sheera felt as if she were swimming up a waterfall, trying to reach the source of his voice, the source of her strength.

"A very wise decision. You are much more sensible than your friend Stanislaus was."

"I thought you said—" Damien began sharply.

"Oh, we got what we wanted from him." Andrzej indicated that he didn't want Jan to put away his knife just yet. "But it took a great deal more, shall we say, 'persuasion,' before he told us what he knew. But then, he had no one he cared about with him." He pinched the tip of Sheera's chin between his thumb and forefinger. "Where is it?" The demand was cold, threatening, ruthless.

"In the tank of a public rest room." Damien sounded hopelessly drained, as if he had been the one who had just lived and died a thousand times, Sheera thought.

"Where?" Andrzej barked.

"On Targowa."

"Good. Very good," he pronounced, the full cheeks rising in a smile.

"And now we can go free?" Sheera asked, trying to keep the tremor out of her voice. She slumped against Damien. His arms went around her protectively.

"Not quite so fast, my pretty little niece-to-be."

She could see why her aunt hated the man on principle alone. Every word out of his mouth sounded loathsome.

"Why not?"

"She is new to the game, is she not?" he asked Damien.

"She has nothing to do with it," Damien snapped back, his arm tightening around her.

"Ah, a dupe. Well, if you must pick one, I commend you on your taste." The reptilian eyes looked her way. "First, we will see if your husband—or lover—here is telling us the truth. Then we will see whether you are free to go or not. And I warn you—" every trace of his smile vanished "—if you are lying, it shall go very badly for you. I am not known for my patience."

He jerked Sheera away from Damien and pushed her out before him. Damien followed, with Jan guarding the rear.

THEY SAT IN THE BLACK LIMOUSINE, waiting, while Jan arrogantly made his way into the ladies' room, several women scattering in his wake.

"He has not yet developed the proper social decorum," Andrzej said, chuckling, as he watched the angry women disperse. "But, with his advantages, he doesn't have to."

She wanted to retort that the only advantages she saw were those that might befit an ape, but she kept her silence, wavering, instead, alternately between fear and rage.

Damien watched Sheera covertly, pretending to look only at the street. He cursed his own "bright" idea for having brought her along. She could have been hurt. She still could be. He hadn't counted on their being detected like this. He had wasted too much time trying not to arouse suspicion. They should have come here the first day and then left quickly. Sometimes, he thought bitterly, scenarios had a way of not working out according to the script. This one certainly wasn't.

It appeared that Andrzej was convinced that Damien was the "main man" and that Sheera's aunt had nothing to do with it. At least that was good. That, plus the designs Andrzej had on Aunt Zosia would keep her safe.

But what would keep them safe?

He wished he could apologize to Sheera. He could tell by the look on her open face that she thought of him as a cold-hearted bastard. But the pose was necessary. The whole ruse was necessary, if they were to have a prayer of staying alive. Damn Bascom. Damn the whole intelligence system. He wished he had seized Sheera that first day, played his instincts and— And what? He was what he was. And he would see the job through.

Not if you're dead, buddy.

Jan abruptly opened the door, shoving his large frame into the car, unmindful that he was crushing Sheera into her seat.

"You have it?" Andrzej asked.

Jan produced the cellophane-wrapped document, grinning like a triumphant five-year-old.

"Good." Andrzej took it from him.

"Now can we leave?" Sheera demanded. Her hostility flared. There was no use in being polite and hoping to win the man's sympathies. He had none.

"You are very naive, Sheera."

Did that mean he was going to kill them after all? Sheera stifled a shiver that threatened to convulse her entire body.

"First, we must have this authenticated."

They were going to die.

She clutched at Damien's hand and he squeezed it. Fat lot of good that did, she thought ruefully.

Andrzej never let them out of the car. Instead, he left them there with the driver and Jan while he went to an annex of the Palace of Culture and Science.

He was going to have the document verified, Sheera thought glumly. And then he was going to come out raging and have them drawn and quartered, or shot, or whatever it was he did with people who didn't cooperate. She knew that Damien would probably die before he'd let them know the information he had stored in his head. There was nothing she could do about that, even if she were inclined to deal with Andrzej. Which she wasn't.

She knew that not allowing them to get the information they were after was for the best, and that frustrated her even more. She would have preferred to feel resentful and justifiably outraged, but she knew that the formula in the document presented a threat not only to her, but to millions of people like her, people who cherished freedom and who did not want to live under the mantle of oppression. People like Judy and Steven and the kids.

Judy. She'd never see her sister again. She'd never see anyone again. She fought back the tears that were gathering in her eyes.

If this had been a movie, something would have been happening right now. Her aunt would have come flying in, bringing in the Resistance fighters she had worked with during the war. Or the nun in the airport would come rushing in, a herald of angels or militant priests at her side. But this was real life and there was no one on the streets who shouldn't have been there. No help. No hope. She pressed her head against the dark window.

You're getting delirious.

She nearly fell out as the door opened.

"Groveling at my feet would not accomplish anything, my dear." Andrzej eased his considerable bulk into the car. She was surprised to hear him sound so pleased with himself. Was it just the calm before the storm? The cobra smiling just before it struck with its poisonous fangs?

"Because I am a generous man," Andrzej said expansively, "and because of the regard I bear for your aunt, you are free to go."

Sheera couldn't believe her ears. He was speaking English, but he might as well have lapsed into Chinese. She stared at him, uncomprehending. He didn't have the formula—or whatever it was called—did he? No, of course not. Why was he letting them go?

"I see you are surprised. Contrary to what you might be thinking, I am not a merciless animal. Besides, ridding oneself of Americans is always troublesome. If you were Hungarians..." He let his voice trail off, letting Sheera fill in the gap with her imagination.

"You're actually letting us go?" Sheera asked incredulously, as if he hadn't said a word.

"Your husband has led us to what we seek. There is no need to resort to bloodshed. Let this be a lesson to others that follow." He enjoyed the last statement, as if he had just uttered a parable to be passed on to posterity. "I will take you to the airport personally—to ensure, shall we say, no further contact with anyone?"

The malevolent smile had returned, but Sheera was past the point of trying to interpret its meaning. What would happen would happen. She just prayed that it would be over with quickly. She wasn't very brave when it came to torture.

When they arrived at Okęcie Airport, Sheera couldn't believe her eyes. He really had brought them to the airport! She looked at Damien, confusion and joy mingling in her features. They were safe; they were being allowed to go home.

She looked back at Andrzej, expecting something to happen.

"Do not look so frightened. I do not care for pretty women to be frightened of me." Sheera's skin began to crawl as he touched her cheek. "When you write to your aunt of this, and I'm sure you shall, be sure to tell her how kind I was to you and your, um, husband."

Sheera drew her courage to her. "About my aunt," she began.

"No harm will come to her because of your stupidity. I have, how would you say, a fancy for her." His expression sombered. He tapped Jan on the shoulder. "Make sure they get on the plane."

"Our passports," Sheera exclaimed suddenly. Hers had been stripped from her, just as her clothes had been.

The pudgy hand delved into the pin-striped jacket, producing two dark items. "Right here."

"And my purse?"

"You have my sympathies, my friend," he said to Damien. "She has the makings of a demanding female." A glint entered his eyes. "But she probably makes up for it in bed, eh?" When Damien didn't answer, Andrzej shrugged, unaffected. "Some things have to be borne patiently." He turned back to her. "Jan will give you your belongings."

They lost no time in getting out. Sheera couldn't fully believe that they were actually being allowed to go free. True to Andrzej's word, Jan held Sheera's purse and the two suitcases, now shoddily taped together, in his ham-like hands.

He ushered them into the terminal like a disgruntled shepherd herding two troublesome sheep.

"Don't you want to freshen up?" Damien asked Sheera as they walked past the rest rooms.

"What?" It seemed an inconceivable time for him to be making such a suggestion.

He fixed her with a patient look. "I just thought you might want to fix your makeup or change your blouse." He touched the rumpled collar. "It's a mess."

"It's probably a lot better than anything in my suitcase." She realized that he was looking at her intently. What was he trying to tell her now? To escape through the window again? No, it couldn't be that. They were trying to get on that plane, not run away from it.

The suitcase. He wanted her to do something with the suitcase.

Okay, but what?

"Yes, maybe I had better," she agreed. She turned to Jan, putting her hand on the suitcase in his grip. "Is it all right?" she asked in Polish.

Jan said nothing. But he saw no harm in her taking it, so he released it.

Damien followed suit. This time, Jan's dull features took on a tinge of suspicion. Damien said to Sheera, "Tell him that the giant who interrogated me forgot to give me my jockey shorts back when he conducted his explorations before. I'd like to put a pair on now."

A hysterical giggle welled up in Sheera's throat. They had almost been killed and he was talking about jockey shorts. She translated Damien's statement.

Jan grunted, letting Damien take the suitcase.

Sheera hurried into the first available stall. She put her suitcase on the seat. Quickly, she searched through the rumpled clothes, pushing things aside. What did Damien think was in there?

She stopped, horrified. A tiny white packet filled with something that might have passed for laundry detergent sat innocuously among her garments.

"Why, that bastard!"

Andrzej wasn't going to do away with them. But he wasn't above letting someone else do it for him. She heaped every curse she could think of on his bald head.

She tossed aside her suitcase and flushed the contents of the packet down the toilet. She let out a tremendous sigh of relief. "Thank God for Damien," she said to herself.

What was she saying? If it hadn't been for Damien, she'd be in her office right now, listening to Haskell's whiny voice drone on and on....

Instead, you've been more alive in the past few days than you've ever been before.

And you are going to stay alive.

There was nothing else planted in her suitcase. Sheera swiftly changed her blouse, knowing that Jan was not above coming in and hauling her out. When she walked back out, Damien was already there. She smiled in answer to his questioning look.

"Ready," she declared.

This time, Jan decided to let them carry their own luggage.

"DO YOU HAVE anything you wish to declare?" the customs official asked in halting English as he looked at her battered case dubiously.

Only that I want desperately to go home, she thought impatiently. She shook her head in answer to his question, then saw the way he was looking at her suitcase. "It fell off the taxi and another car hit it," she explained, feeling strangely euphoric now that it was all over.

All over. Was it all over? Was it all over between them, too, she wondered sneaking a look at Damien.

The customs offical sifted through her belongings, then waved her on.

She turned to look over her shoulder, half expecting Jan to come loping after them like a clumsy Saint Bernard, ready to retrieve them for his master.

But Jan stayed where he was, watching them walk toward the plane. Obviously, Andrzej had instructed him to stay until the end and report back. And, just as obviously, Sheera thought with relief, he hadn't told Jan what to expect. So he was not suspicious when the customs officials let them pass.

Her knees felt like water.

She continued to worry, feeling weak and tense, until after takeoff. At any moment, she felt, Andrzej would come running into the plane to drag them off.

But he never did.

ANDRZEJ SAT in his limousine, watching the plane take off. They had outsmarted him, he thought, grudgingly doffing his hat to them. But no matter. He had what he wanted. And they would be taken care of once they landed. Another matter closed.

He instructed the driver to take him back.

"I DON'T UNDERSTAND," Sheera said once they were airborne. "Why did he let us go?"

"He didn't, really. By planting that—"

She waved that explanation aside. "I know, I know. What I mean is—" she glanced around, lowering her voice to the point of being almost inaudible "—the document. He brought it to the Palace of Culture. Wouldn't one of the scientists have realized that he didn't have the correct document?"

"But he did."

Sheera stared at him, totally lost. "Were we decoys, then? Who *are* you working for, anyway?"

He slipped his hand over hers, deriving as much comfort from the action as he hoped he gave. "We weren't decoys. He has the first part of the formula—"

"But then—"

"Without," Damien continued, "a few pertinent factors. This way, they'll think that we don't have the second half and lost our bid at getting the first. Ergo, we have nothing and they go on thinking that their plans are safe."

"What do you mean 'safe'? I thought we had the only copy."

He shook his head. "With something of this magnitude, we can only assume that several copies exist."

"Then getting the second half didn't really accomplish anything," she said, dejected. All this was for nothing? "Not if they still have the plans."

"On the contrary, now at least we're even. The balance of power goes on, and the world gets to exist for another day or so, until the next crisis," he ended philosophically.

Sheera felt as if she were collapsing against her cushion. "You think of everything, don't you?"

"Not me." He laughed modestly. "Bascom."

She turned to him, her head cradled against the headrest. "What made you think Andrzej had planted something in our suitcases?"

"I know his type," he answered lightly. "He didn't want our blood on his hands, but that didn't mean he wasn't willing to pass us on to someone else."

"As he said, he's a generous man."

A flight attendant came by and asked if they wanted something to drink. Sheera ordered three gin-and-tonics.

"I wouldn't do that if I were you," Damien said after the woman walked away, a bemused expression on her face.

"But you're not me," Sheera pointed out. "And some of us don't have nerves of steel."

"You were magnificent," he told her.

"I was scared out of my mind."

"You hid it well."

I hide a lot of things well, she thought ruefully, wondering if he knew the way she felt about him.

She liked the sound of his praise. At least, if nothing else, she told herself, she had gained his respect. She hadn't folded, hadn't broken under the strain. She had allowed Damien to play out his little melodrama, adding the right touches of authenticity to it to make Andrzej believe it.

"And what happens now?" Sheera asked as the flight attendant returned with her drinks.

"Now we reinstate you into your peaceful life."

The words brought a terrible wave of depression to her. She downed the first drink quickly.

Chapter Eighteen

Sheera struggled to put her feelings in order. It was a difficult chore. Even the long flight back to Kennedy Airport hadn't provided her with enough time to sort out her emotions. The pieces surrounding the mission had all fallen into place, or as much as they were going to. But the pieces of her life, well, that was another matter. Once they landed, Damien wouldn't need her anymore. Would he want to keep on seeing her? Shipboard romances had a way of floundering on land. Could the same be said for spy romances? A rueful smile played across her lips.

"Finally smiling," Damien said as the plane was landing. "I was beginning to think that the incident with Andrzej had made you forget how to smile; I wouldn't have wanted that on my conscience."

How would you like a broken heart on your conscience, she thought, still smiling glibly.

"Excited about going home?" he asked.

"Excited about going anywhere," she answered. "For a while there, I thought that that was it." She turned to face him squarely. "I thought that hulking KGB agent was going to kill me right in front of your unblinking eyes." She knew it sounded like an accusation, but she couldn't help herself. The thought had been festering within her since Jan had held her in his grip.

"My eyes didn't blink for a reason. I was trying to call Andrzej's bluff."

"Some bluff," she scoffed. "He could have killed me."

"He wouldn't have."

"What makes you so sure?" she challenged.

"Because I would have killed him first," he said, the calm in his voice masking his true emotions.

"How?" The idea of him acting as her protector did wonderful things to her flagging composure.

"With my bare hands." His expression was somber. "I'm sorry you had to go all through that."

But she didn't want him to be sorry, not about having her along. "Now that it's over," she conceded, "I've got to admit, it was rather exciting. When you look at things in retrospect, you tend to leave out the worst and include the best."

Her somber look faded and he brightened. "That's the way I usually feel. It's what keeps this job from getting routine."

What a wonderful way to get your blood going in the morning, she thought cryptically, knowing you had death to look forward to.

"Murphy will be waiting for us at the airport," he told her as the seat-belt sign flashed off. "We'll drop you off first."

"Oh, yes, of course." Her voice sounded hollow, stilted. He couldn't wait to get rid of her. Excess baggage, to be left off at the nearest stop. She wanted desperately to ask him if she would ever see him again. But she couldn't. She had done all the pursuing from the beginning. It was up to him now.

Damien looked at her curiously. "Something the matter?"

"No, just tired," she lied. "I need a hot bath. I think I'll stay in the tub for a week."

Damien smiled, envisioning her soaking in a tub, bubbles dissolving a little at a time, revealing enticing contours that he had vividly committed to memory. There were some definite advantages to having a photographic memory.

"Sounds inviting," he murmured. "Am I?"

"Are you what?" As usual, he had lost her. The plane had come to a stop and the people were gathering their belongings and moving into the crowded aisle. She fumbled with her seat belt.

"Invited."

She was halfway into the aisle and turned to stare at him. People kept pushing past her. After the long flight, tempers were frayed and several passengers glared at her for blocking their exit. "Would you like to be?"

He smiled at her, his eyes taking on an unbearably sensuous gleam. "Guess."

No, she wasn't taking a chance on making a fool of herself. She'd taken enough risks to last her a lifetime. "I'm too tired to guess. Tell me."

"Yes, I would like to be."

Suddenly, she wasn't tired anymore. Joy pumped adrenaline through her veins as she took his face in both her hands and kissed him soundly. "You've just earned yourself a season's pass to my private spa." She gave him a sexy smile. "I have a sunken tub."

He held her in his arms, unmindful of the stares they were garnering. "I never made love in a sunken tub before."

Sheera shook her head, feigning disappointment. "And here I thought you were so sophisticated."

The taste of that first kiss stirred Damien to repeat the performance. Ignoring the disembarking people as they jabbed them with their bodies and carry-on luggage, Damien pulled Sheera closer, kissing her passionately.

Sheera felt a combination of relief and ecstasy in his kiss, matching her mood exactly. The emotions she had held in check earlier, while frightful things had been happening to her, combined with the thought of what could have happened to her, now exploded into an almost overwhelming desire.

Someone was tapping her on the shoulder. At first lightly, then more insistently. Sheera blinked, tearing herself away from Damien and his intoxicating mouth.

"I'm afraid you're going to have to get off," a sweet-voiced flight attendant told her. She gave Sheera a long, envious look.

"I'm not afraid." Sheera laughed, taking Damien's hand securely in her own. "I'm not afraid of anything anymore."

"You certainly have perked up," Damien commented as they made their way off the plane. They were the last to leave.

"The promise of a bubble bath always has that kind of effect on me," she tossed gaily over her shoulder as they hurried down the long ramp.

Damien laughed. "Something tells me I'm going to wind up with the pruniest woman in Manhattan. Lucky for you, I love prunes." He captured a bit of her earlobe in a swift kiss just before they merged with the milling crowd at the ground floor of the airport. Sheera turned to kiss him again.

She had no idea how he managed it, but Murphy appeared almost magically at their side.

Sheera withdrew her arms from about Damien's neck. "Hello, Murphy. Here we are, back at last." She was feeling positively giddy, she thought as she gave the man's fat cheek a quick kiss. Everything was beautiful. She was free, happy and in love. What more could she possibly ask for?

"The regional director wants to see you as soon as possible. He's waiting at the Claremont Hotel," Murphy said to Damien in a hushed voice. "I'm to bring you as soon as you land."

"Well, I've landed," Damien said, resigning himself to another long, verbose ordeal before he could take Sheera up on her invitation. But that was to be expected. Delay made the getting that much sweeter, he thought. Absently, he wondered what the regional director was doing at the Claremont, but then, things were never orthodox in his profession.

"The car's this way." Murphy led them through the throng of well-wishers and tearful people who were either coming or going, or staying behind.

"Do I at least get a chance to change?" Damien asked Murphy as they went out into the parking lot. "I've looked better."

His suit was rumpled and his jacket was torn in places. Sheera thought she had never seen a more compelling sight.

"He said to hurry," Murphy answered nervously.

"Why?" It didn't make any sense. Surely they could spare half an hour.

"That he didn't say."

That sounded typical, Damien thought irritably. "This won't be long," he promised Sheera.

Murphy looked flustered. "Is she coming with us?"

"Yes, why?" He was surprised at Murphy's reaction. Murphy never questioned him.

"Well, I thought that maybe she could take a cab..." the other man began lamely.

"Decidedly unfriendly of you, Murphy. We've just been to hell and back together." He squeezed Sheera against him affectionately. "I can't ask her to pay her own cab fare. It wouldn't seem ethical." With that, he ushered her into the BMW.

"No time to stop anyplace?" Sheera asked, snuggling up against Damien. God, he felt so warm, so wonderful. She could stay like this forever. She leaned forward and playfully half-whispered the amorous invitation Damien had insisted on learning in Polish.

Her eyes had drifted dreamily toward the front when she saw Murphy's startled reaction in the rearview mirror.

He understood!

Sheera was willing to bet her life on it. His eyes bore the mark of unmistakable comprehension.

Damien felt her body stiffen next to his. "What is it?"

"Nothing." She shook her head so hard that it hurt. She saw Murphy watching her warily.

"Look out!" Damien cried as a station wagon swerved to avoid their car. The BMW had drifted into the next lane.

"Sorry," Murphy muttered. "Not enough sleep lately."

"Murphy, do you still have that room at the hotel?" Sheera asked suddenly, her mind racing a mile a minute, wisps of frantic, unformed ideas floating about. She tried to keep her voice calm.

"Yes, Cari's there, but—"

"Could we go there?" Sheera asked, switching her focus to Damien. "Please?"

She looked so petulant, he felt his blood stirring even more. Damn rules and regulations. "All right, Sheera, right after I see—"

"No, now," she insisted, her eyes pleading with him.

"Sheera, you heard Murphy. I have to—"

"Please, Damien?"

This was no whimsical request on her part. Something was wrong. A moment ago, she was whispering sweet nothings into his ear—conveniently in Polish, so that Murphy wouldn't understand—and now she was acting like a cat on a hot tin roof. What had triggered it? He saw Murphy looking at them in the rearview mirror. The look was exceedingly wary. Murphy probably thought that Sheera had been brainwashed back there, or worse. Murphy was always a worrier.

"Tell me what's wrong, Sheera," Damien said patiently, taking her hands into his.

She pressed her lips together in frustration. She couldn't say anything in front of Murphy. There was no telling where he would take them, or what he would do. He had the wheel. Ipso facto, he had control. She felt as stymied as when Damien told her to go to the bathroom at the airport.

The bathroom! That was it!

"I have to go to the bathroom!" she announced rather loudly.

It wasn't the kind of thing Damien expected her to announce publicly. "I would have thought you'd have your fill of ladies' rooms by now," he said with a short laugh.

"No." She shook her head, copper curls bouncing in all directions. "I have to go. Now."

Damien sighed. She was acting really odd. He decided to give her her lead. "Find the lady a gas station, Murphy."

"We'll be late," Murphy protested.

"I'll explain," Damien protested. Sheera didn't relax. Instead, she gripped his hand tightly. Was she trying to tell him something? Why wasn't she saying it, then? Was she afraid of Murphy? But why, for God's sake? And what was there to tell him? All that remained was for him to write down what he knew, unlock the secret of his mind and be done with it.

"Will this one do?" Murphy asked, coming to a stop at a run-down station just off the expressway. The station sign boasted of the lowest prices in the neighborhood.

Sheera frowned. "It looks a little seedy."

Damien could have sworn she sounded happy about it.

"Come with me," she asked Damien suddenly. "To stand outside the door," she explained quickly, darting a look at Murphy.

"Be right back," Damien told the man as he slid out. "All right," he fell into step with Sheera, "what's this all about?"

She didn't answer until they rounded a corner of the station and were out of sight. "He knows."

Her words were out of left field. "He? Who's he?"

"Murphy."

"Murphy? What does Murphy know?"

"Polish. He understood me," she insisted urgently.

The lines in his jaw tightened. Amusement totally erased. Damien gripped both her shoulders. "What makes you say that?"

She knew he didn't like hearing this. "He understood what I just said to you. I could see it in his eyes. In the rearview mirror," she clarified, her thoughts running together.

"But if he understands, why didn't he come forward when we needed a translator?"

"I don't know. That's your department. I'm only telling you what I know. What I feel," she amended. She didn't know, not really. "But when I spoke to you in Polish, he jerked his head up. He *knew* what I was saying," she insisted.

Murphy. She had to be wrong. Murphy had trained him. Murphy had been there for him countless times. Yet the KGB had known about Stan's being in Warsaw. Someone had told Andrzej about it. They also knew all about Sheera's being there. There was no way Stan could have told Andrzej about Sheera. Stan didn't know about Sheera.

But Murphy did. And Murphy could gain access to her dossier.

It was a bitter pill to swallow.

"You stay here," Damien instructed, physically pushing her against the wall.

"Why?" she demanded. "What are you going to do?"

"Find out if you're right."

"If I am, he's dangerous."

"Yes," he agreed grimly. He stepped out cautiously to see what Murphy was doing.

Sheera grabbed his arm. "God, don't walk off like John Wayne for a shoot-out. Maybe we can distract him."

"I don't think that's necessary." Maybe he could reason with him.

Murphy was standing with his back to them, eyeing his wristwatch nervously, a cigarette dangling absently from his lips. He didn't like this. Any of it. When he received that phone call in his apartment early that morning, the voice on the other end had been explicit. His orders were clear. Bring Damien to them.

He didn't want to think about what they wanted Damien for. Damn the circumstances that had done this to him. Damn his own cowardly obsession with Lily. Another man would have walked away from it all. Another man would have kept his pride. But he wasn't like any other man. He was Jozef Antoni Murphy, a man caught in the middle, a man whose conscience was troubling him more and more. It had taken him two full days to get his hands on Sheera's dossier to find out the name of the aunt they were staying with in Warsaw. And he hadn't wanted to relay the information to Andrzej, but he had gotten in too deep not to.

"Why, Murphy?" Damien asked, surprising him from behind.

Murphy whirled around. "Why what?"

"Why did you sell out?"

"What are you talking about?" Murphy laughed. It was a nervous laugh. His cigarette fell from his mouth.

Slowly, Damien walked around the car's hood. "You were never any good at lying, Murph. That's why they always left you with the paperwork." He moved to grasp his friend's hand. "It's no good."

Murphy wrenched free from Damien's lax hold. "I never thought it was," he admitted mournfully. Rather than draw for his service revolver, he bolted.

Damien ran after him, and they rounded the corner to the self-service island, where a man was replacing the gas cap on his Porsche. Murphy pushed him out of the way, slid behind the wheel and peeled out.

Damien doubled back and headed for the BMW.

"Oh, no, you don't," Sheera cried, "not without me." She managed to hop into the car just as it began moving.

"You idiot, you could get killed leaping into a moving car!"

"Then you should have slowed down," she gasped, pulling herself into an upright position. "I was strip-searched because of you. If you think I'm going to let you run off now, you're crazy."

"This isn't exactly a joyride I'm on," he pointed out grimly.

"Yes," she said quietly, sensing the way he felt, "I know."

The expressway was beginning to get crowded, but not enough to impede their progress. The red Porsche wove in and out of the traffic. Cars screeched and swerved to avoid colliding with it. Damien was gaining on him.

"Got my training driving in L.A.," Damien confided dryly, his eyes fixed on the Porsche. *Why, Murphy, why?* The thought kept hammering at his brain. What made a good man sell out?

Sheera gripped the side of the front seat, trying to keep her stomach from lurching forward. "Glad to hear that," she muttered. Her eyes grew wide as she watched the road. "Oh, God, Damien, there's a gasoline truck up ahead! He's heading straight for it!"

Her words were barely out when it happened. The driver of the tanker truck tried to move his rig out of the way, but it was too late. The Porsche crashed into the truck's side, almost as if Murphy had done it on purpose. Flames began shooting out.

Damien pulled over to the shoulder. Sheera buried her head on his shoulder, keeping a sob from tearing from her throat by pressing her hands over her mouth.

"Damien, I'm so sorry."

"You have nothing to be sorry about. You probably saved our lives," he said, his voice calm, numb. He sat in his seat, gripping the steering wheel, staring out at the bright orange-and-blue flames that engulfed the sports car. "My guess is, he was taking us to his superior, not mine."

He sighed, dropping his head forward for a moment. Sheera searched for something to say but could find no words of comfort.

"C'mon," he said, steering the car to the nearest exit, "we still have to get to headquarters."

SHEERA SAT in the cold, antiseptic hallway, counting the number of tiles that went from her hard wooden bench to the elevator. She had been sitting there long enough for the muscles in her posterior to plead for her to assume a different position. She stared at the frosty glass door that separated her from Damien and Bascom, wondering what was going on.

People passed her, giving her only a cursory glance. Actually, they were giving her badge a cursory glance. The word "Visitor" was stamped on it. Damien had pinned it to her chest and glibly told her that the badge would keep her from being carried off.

She thought of that last time she had been carried off, and she hung on to the badge for dear life, fingering it from time to time to make sure it was still there.

How long did making a report take?

She looked at her watch. She had translated the document for him in less time than this. But he had a full verbal report to deliver. And they probably had questions to ask. She could be there all night.

That was all right. She was prepared to wait. She could wait for him forever.

DAMIEN PUT THE PEN DOWN on Bascom's desk. "That's it," he said, sighing.

Bascom, a thin, sallow-faced man, picked up the sheets and looked them over carefully. "Looks like gibberish to me."

"That's what she said."

"She?"

"Sheera O'Malley."

"Oh, yes." Bascom's mind held a sea of names. "Worked out well, didn't it?"

"Very well."

There was something in his tone that made Bascom look up and then smile. "Yes, I've seen her picture in the dossier. Well, you're free to go." He turned his swivel chair around, reaching for his phone. Damien was still standing there. "Yes?"

"About Murphy," Damien began slowly.

Bascom sighed. "A real pity. Don't know what makes a good man like that go sour. Heard that his new wife ran up a tab that rivaled the national debt, but I always thought that was just jealous hearsay. She's some looker." He cleared his throat. "So they tell me."

Poor Murphy. The wrong choices all the way.

"Could we keep his name out of it?" Damien asked.

"That's highly irregular."

"I knew him better than anyone, or, at least," Damien corrected ruefully, shoving his hands into his pockets, "I thought I did. He was a government man all the way."

"Shame he switched governments midstream." Bascom drew on his pipe. He wasn't oblivious to Damien's feelings. "I'll see what I can do."

"Thanks." Damien turned to leave.

"And, Conrad..."

Damien stopped short at the door. "Yes?"

"Tell Miss O'Malley we're grateful."

Damien grinned. "I'll convey the message."

"Yes—" Bascom smiled to himself as he rocked in his chair, puffing on his pipe "—I daresay you will."

Sheera leaped to her feet as soon as Damien came out the door. "Are you through?"

"With the report? Yes. With you, no."

"Got another mission for me?" she asked teasingly.

"Yes, relaxing a tense agent."

"Ah, my private spa."

"Exactly." He led her to the elevator, exactly ninety-two tiles away from her bench. "Have any brandy?" He jabbed the "down" button.

"I might be able to find some. What'll we drink to?" she wanted to know as they got in.

"Us, for openers. Sorry, private elevator," he said to the man coming up behind them. The man stared at them, bewildered, as the doors closed. "Our future," he told her, taking her into his arms.

"Future?" Sheera echoed. "Do we have a future?"

"Well, you're not out of danger yet, you know."

"More KGB?" she asked as the express elevator took them to the ground floor.

"Possibly. You never know in this business. I might have to put in some more hours guarding that luscious body of yours."

"How many more hours?" she asked as the elevator came to a stop. She made no move to get out.

"I'm not sure. How many hours are there in a lifetime?"

"Are you asking me...?" She gasped, unable to finish the sentence.

"Sounds like it, doesn't it?"

"Marriage?"

"Easiest way to mix business with pleasure," he told her. "And, lady, I sure mean business."

They were probably the first couple ever to kiss passionately in the elevator of that particular government agency, Sheera thought, standing on her toes as she wrapped her arms about his neck. Not a bad way to go down in history at that.

The elevator door closed, taking them for another ride.

HARLEQUIN FIRST·CLASS Sweepstakes

OFFICIAL RULES

1. NO PURCHASE NECESSARY. To enter, complete the official entry/order form. Be sure to indicate whether or not you wish to take advantage of our subscription offer.

2. Entry blanks have been preselected for the prizes offered. Your response will be checked to see if you are a winner. In the event that these preselected responses are not claimed, a random drawing will be held from all entries received to award not less than $150,000 in prizes. This is in addition to any free, surprise or mystery gifts which might be offered. Versions of this sweepstakes with different prizes will appear in Preview Service Mailings by Harlequin Books and their affiliates. Winners selected will receive the prize offered in their sweepstakes brochure.

3. This promotion is being conducted under the supervision of Marden-Kane, an independent judging organization. By entering the sweepstakes, each entrant accepts and agrees to be bound by these rules and the decisions of the judges, which shall be final and binding. Odds of winning in the random drawing are dependent upon the total number of entries received. Taxes, if any, are the sole responsibility of the prize winners. Prizes are nontransferable. All entries must be received by August 31, 1986.

4. The following prizes will be awarded:

    (1) Grand Prize: Rolls-Royce™ *or* $100,000 Cash!
    (Rolls-Royce being offered by permission of Rolls-Royce Motors Inc.)

    (1) Second Prize: A trip for two to Paris for 7 days/6 nights. Trip includes air transportation on the Concorde, hotel accommodations...PLUS...$5,000 spending money!

    (1) Third Prize: A luxurious Mink Coat!

5. This offer is open to residents of the U.S. and Canada, 18 years or older, except employees of Harlequin Books, its affiliates, subsidiaries, Marden-Kane and all other agencies and persons connected with conducting this sweepstakes. All Federal, State and local laws apply. Void in the province of Quebec and wherever prohibited or restricted by law. Winners will be notified by mail and may be required to execute an affidavit of eligibility and release, which must be returned within 14 days after notification. Canadian winners will be required to answer a skill-testing question. Winners consent to the use of their name, photograph and/or likeness for advertising and publicity purposes in conjunction with this and similar promotions without additional compensation. One prize per family or household.

6. For a list of our most current prize winners, send a stamped, self-addressed envelope to: WINNERS LIST, c/o Marden-Kane, P.O. Box 10404, Long Island City, New York 11101

SWRL·A·1

WORLDWIDE LIBRARY IS YOUR TICKET TO ROMANCE, ADVENTURE AND EXCITEMENT

Experience it all in these big, bold Bestsellers— Yours exclusively from WORLDWIDE LIBRARY WHILE QUANTITIES LAST

To receive these Bestsellers, complete the order form, detach and send together with your check or money order (include 75¢ postage and handling), payable to WORLDWIDE LIBRARY, to:

In the U.S.
WORLDWIDE LIBRARY
Box 52040
Phoenix, AZ
85072-2040

In Canada
WORLDWIDE LIBRARY
P.O. Box 2800, 5170 Yonge Street
Postal Station A, Willowdale, Ontario
M2N 6J3

Quant.	Title	Price
_____	**ANTIGUA KISS**, Anne Weale	$2.95
_____	**WILD CONCERTO**, Anne Mather	$2.95
_____	**STORMSPELL**, Anne Mather	$2.95
_____	**A VIOLATION**, Charlotte Lamb	$3.50
_____	**LEGACY OF PASSION**, Catherine Kay	$3.50
_____	**SECRETS**, Sheila Holland	$3.50
_____	**SWEET MEMORIES**, LaVyrle Spencer	$3.50
_____	**FLORA**, Anne Weale	$3.50
_____	**SUMMER'S AWAKENING**, Anne Weale	$3.50
_____	**FINGER PRINTS**, Barbara Delinsky	$3.50
_____	**DREAMWEAVER**, Felicia Gallant/Rebecca Flanders	$3.50
_____	**EYE OF THE STORM**, Maura Seger	$3.50
_____	**HIDDEN IN THE FLAME**, Anne Mather	$3.50
	YOUR ORDER TOTAL	$_____
	New York and Arizona residents add appropriate sales tax	$_____
	Postage and Handling	$ .75
	I enclose	$_____

NAME _____

ADDRESS _____ APT.# _____

CITY _____

STATE/PROV. _____ ZIP/POSTAL CODE _____

WW2